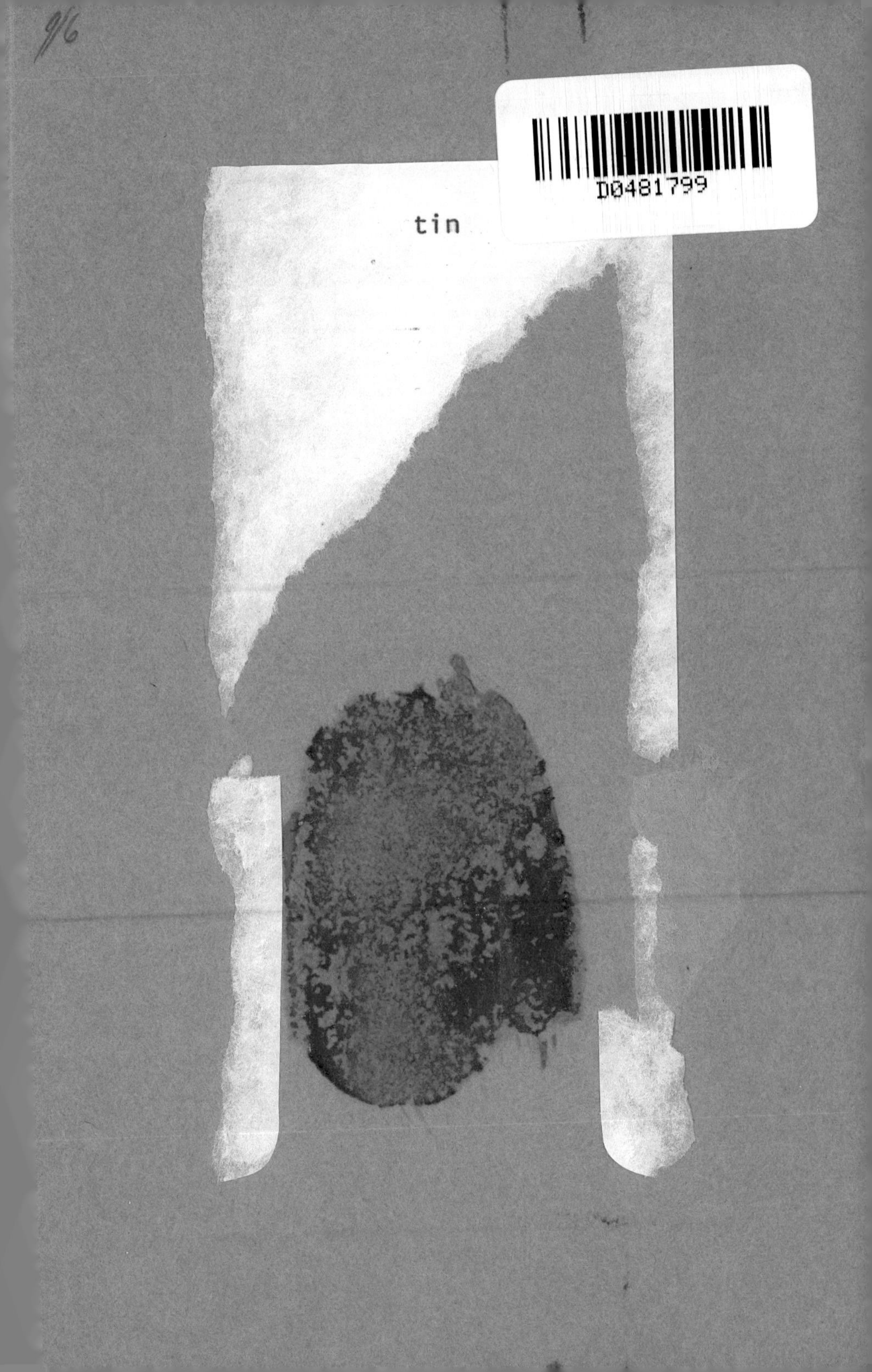

tin
D0481799

for Veronica

Tree Frog

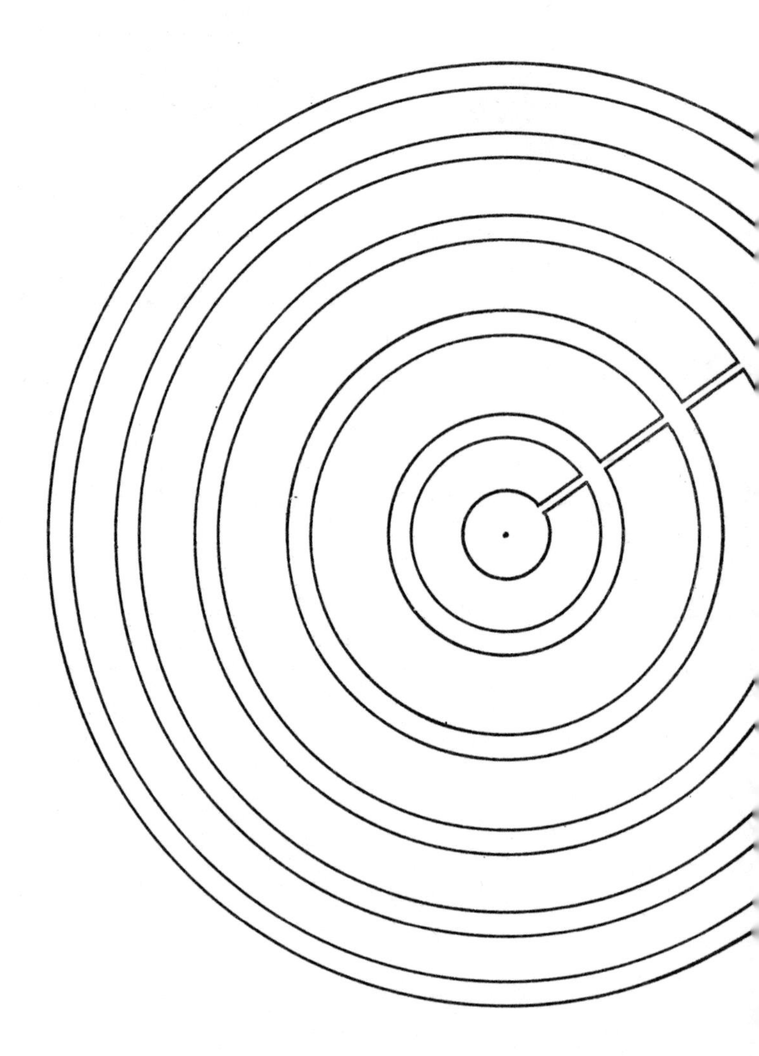

TREE FROG

MARTIN WOODHOUSE

Coward-McCann, Inc.
New York

First American Edition 1966

Second Impression

Library of Congress Catalog
Card Number: 66-16581

PRINTED IN THE UNITED STATES OF AMERICA

Prologue

I WAS in my coffin. Why had they buried me face downward?

Seconds passed, and I became conscious that I was breathing. Events had been catching up with me too fast. Was I back in the trunk of that car?

The mind moves slowly, sorting out these things. At first I believed I could see nothing, that I was pressed down upon nothing, upon velvet a hundred fathoms deep, upon the floor of a tomb. I put out my tongue, and tasted plastic, like sucking the angle of a set square in fourth-form physics class.

Sometimes the mind cannot sort things out at all.

Far-off night shapes drifted in front of my eyes, and I knew where I was. Everything that had been said and done led to this exact moment. I knew that too.

I should have done my homework. It is all very well complaining now, but there are definitions in intelligence work as precise as those I use in science, and if I'd paid more attention to Sloane I'd have known and understood those definitions weeks ago. Tree Frog was a deception operation.

TREE FROG

8

I waited for someone to speak. Logically, they had to speak. But it was only when I was sure that, after all, they wouldn't, that I'd been left alone, that this was part of it too, that I heard Andy's voice whispering in my ear.

Tree Frog

One

"THEY aren't going to wear it, you know," said Michaelson. "That's a fact. Or as near to a fact as you can get."

"What you mean, sir," I said, "is that you aren't even going to put it up to them."

He went on looking out of the window. I could see that it was going to be one of those days. Michaelson was being Julius Caesar and I was bored stiff, but I had all the time in the world. Research gets to be a bit like that some days. You come in to work three minutes early and spend the next hour and a half with your chin in your hands wondering what to do next, and why you aren't somewhere else like industry.

"I didn't say that."

He came away from the window and foraged around on his desk. The elongated wooden prism bearing his name on one facet and on another the words DIRECTOR OF RESEARCH fell to the floor with a clatter. I picked it up. We all had these objects in case, as McTeague suggested, we forgot who we were or how far up the ladder we'd clawed our way. I turned Michaelson's over in my hand to see if he'd got anything unprintable on the third surface, but he hadn't, unlike McTeague, who was retarded even for a scientist. I replaced it on the desk and straightened up. Michaelson was scrutinizing my budget application form closely, as though for furniture beetles.

"All I said was that Admiralty may—in fact they will—disallow your figure for computer time. Twelve hundred pounds is too much, far too much. I don't know what you can have been thinking of. I couldn't even use it as a bargaining figure. You must see that, Giles."

"What will they suggest, then?" I asked.

"You know quite well. What they always suggest. They'll see our staff list. They'll say that we've got three statisticians—"

"With desk calculators."

"With desk calculators, granted. I'm only pointing out what they'll say."

I knew we had about five minutes of this sort of mandarin exchange to go through before we got down to the trading game itself. Any moment now he was going to tell me to have a seat, which meant the Design Center chair in front of the desk, the one which made you feel as though you were actually sitting below floor level. In order to forestall this I propped myself cautiously against the desk itself. He frowned slightly.

"The last time it arose," I said, "they frigged it so that I went round to the University math department cap in hand to cadge some free time on *their* computer. Well, that isn't going to work now. They're not giving away computer time any more, as of last month. That twelve hundred represents the amount they're going to cane us for even supposing they'll let us use it at all. They've got work of their own to do."

"Is that true?" He seemed surprised. Seemed.

"I'm afraid so, director."

"Miss Abrams—"

"No. Not Binnie. Look, sir, do you know what we pay those girls in Stats? If we use Binnie it'll take four months solid. I know it looks as though we got her time thrown in with a pound of tea, but we don't. My calculations show . . ." It was my turn to scrabble around for bits of paper. Michaelson surveyed me benignly.

"Don't bother, Giles."

I stopped. Michaelson sat down, all sweet reason for the moment. We both knew what I was going to say next, but that didn't stop me saying it.

"If we had our own computer it would be different."

He screwed up his mouth thoughtfully. All he was trying to do was pick a line of defense—there were four that I could think of unless he'd worked out a brand new one in his bath since February, which was the last time we had this argument. I hitched myself farther onto the desk and waited. He started to frown again, then threw his eraser into the air several times and caught it.

"So that was the idea," he said.

"What was?"

"This twelve hundred pounds. Now come on, Giles, you don't really want that amount of computer time, what you want is for the Institute to invest in a computer and save itself a lot of money."

He smiled boyishly, which I found even harder to take than the Julius Caesar bit. As though to emphasize his descent to my level, he threw the eraser in the air again, reached back behind his head to catch it and only saved himself from tilting over backward by hooking his toe under the desk leg. He then stood the wooden prism on its end and balanced the eraser on it.

"I suppose if we were to add up all the sums of money you've requested for computer utilization time over the last two years on these things," he brandished my budget form again, "we'd find we couldn't afford to do without one."

"I hope so."

"And where would we put it?"

"In Stats of course. The girls would love it."

"There wouldn't be room, surely, Giles."

I looked at him. I couldn't believe this.

"Computers," I said carefully, "are getting smaller and smaller. We don't have to build an annex, not for the one I have in mind, sir."

"Really?" he said. "I didn't realize that. Perhaps I've been watching too much television recently. I still tend to visualize the things as filling three sides of a room."

I had been trying to persuade Michaelson to ask the powers that be for a computer for three years now. During that period I had completed five projects for the Institute and I was still no nearer to getting one. Project Flittermouse One I'd done the statistics for myself. Flittermouse Two they'd given, in raw data form, to about three hundred Naval writers to thrash out. It took them about six weeks and they gave me the figures back in a printed file that I spent another six weeks trying to understand. It had then been agreed by all and sundry that this particular method wouldn't do, but by then I was immersed in the auditory threshold experiment which thank the Lord, didn't need any complicated math. By the time Flittermouse Three came around my estimated budget for computation was nine hundred (I wouldn't like to try and guess what the Naval writers had cost by the time we were through) and nobody wanted to know again. That was the time McTeague and I had begged, beaten and bribed our way into the Math Department's Computer Section. The two engineers and the astrophysicist we displaced raised such a fuss that we'd had a punitive expedition from higher levels. The interception trials I'd worked out with Binnie Abrams and Laura from Stats. Both the girls were on overtime wages then, clever little things, and Binnie went to Perugia for a month on the profits. I went camping in Wales, being a member of the salaried classes.

I estimated that during the course of an average experiment, the result of which everybody usually knew in advance anyway, I spent a week setting up, a week writing my report and about seven weeks hammering the keys of an electric calculator, and I was getting good and fed up with the whole system. I wanted a computer. But I wasn't going to get it this time either. That was obvious.

"As a matter of interest," said Michaelson, "how big are they nowadays?"

"About the size of a typewriter," I told him.

"Well, when they've got down to the price of a typewriter as well, I'll buy you one," he smiled fleetingly and I knew it was no good. The infuriating thing was that he was only too likely to come breezing into my room tomorrow wheeling a computer on a large trolley, having won it at poker dice with the Establishments Officer or something. This was one of his favorite ways of disarming opposition.

I went back to my room. In the passage outside I met McTeague, who raised his eyebrows, and right thumb, inquiringly. I pushed open my door with my foot and he followed me inside. I slammed around my workbench in silence for a few seconds and he propped himself against the blackboard, watching me. For some obscure reason of his own McTeague treats me as though we were childhood friends. In fact about the only thing we have in common is a reaction against discipline of all kinds and scientific discipline in particular, but I sometimes get the feeling that he expects us to wear lapel badges proclaiming our common membership of the iconoclasts club, which must by now be getting so large that there can be hardly anybody left outside to react against.

"I can see," said McTeague, "that not only did you fail to get your computer but he won the argument hands down."

I looked for a cigarette and sat down.

"Well?" he said.

"Quite right. No computer. Now will you please get out?"

"You'll get ulcers."

"I've already got them."

"I wonder why Michaelson doesn't pick on someone his own size."

"Out, McTeague. And take your bloody rotten lousy stinking bastard sense of humor with you."

He came away from the blackboard and leaned heavily on my desk.

"You know what I'd do if I were you, Giles? I'd go on strike. Let them work out their own figures for a change. It's all a lot of rubbish in any case. You know what I always say—"

"Yes, I do."

"If you need to prove it by statistics, it ain't so. That's what I always say," said McTeague. "What are you going to do about the figures, anyway?"

"Plod through them myself again. Binnie can help me. Maybe this time she can go skiing on her overtime pay."

"Binnie, eh?" He narrowed his eyes. He may have thought he was leering. "What are you in such a foul temper for then? If I was offered a choice between a real live girl and a dead computer for an assistant it wouldn't take me long to make up my mind."

"Look, McTeague." (Nobody ever called McTeague by his first name, I'm not sure why.) "I've got work to do. Haven't you?" I searched around the desk. I couldn't think what I was looking for, but I found I could very quickly have too much of McTeague, especially in his sexual innuendo phase. There's no particular reason why scientific establishments should be any less prone to this sort of thing than any other concentrations of human beings, I suppose, but I wasn't in the mood for it this morning. McTeague headed for the door.

"I can tell when I'm not wanted," he said. "But you're bashing your head against a brick wall where that girl's concerned. Take some fatherly advice."

"Such as?"

"I've got a theory about Binnie."

"I know you have."

"No, this is a new one. You see—"

"I don't want to hear it," I said. "Close the door after you."

A second later he was back. I still hadn't found anything to do.

"I knew there was something," he said.

"What?"

"Well, look. I'm off on my holidays next week."

"And?"

He came back into the room and shut the door. He looked like someone who was about to take me for a pound, and I didn't like it.

"The thing is," he said, "there's an evaluation to do, and I wondered if you'd take it on. I haven't accepted it myself, and if I could put you up as an alternative it would make things a lot easier."

"Who's it for?"

"The Bayswater boys. Chapman."

"Oh God," I said. "Must we? Is it a mucky one?"

"Don't know. I don't think so, though. I mean, you can usually tell by the way Chapman sounds on the phone, can't you? If he's being damned circumspect then it probably is. But he wasn't this time. Bits of plane, he said."

"Or else you're a plausible liar, McTeague."

One of the things we did every now and then was crash evaluation. It was one of the penalties involved in our deal with the Air Ministry whereby we got some futile sum of money which they fought about every year. It didn't happen very often, but when it did, it was usually McTeague, Dinsdale or myself who had to come running, because of our security grading. None of us liked the job. There is an apocryphal story, theory or whatever you like to call it about the Tank Corps. According to the story, during the war members of the Tank Corps were instructed not to go inside disabled or burned-out tanks, on the grounds that being in a tank is great fun while everybody is bouncing off the sides but if you get hit by something that goes straight through you instead, the resulting mess is liable to put even strong silent cavalrymen off for life. I don't believe the theory's true, but it about sums up what we felt about crash evaluations; every so often there was still somebody inside when the plane hit the ground and I didn't attend post-mortems often enough to be inured to it.

"All right," I said. "But if it turns out to be bits and pieces of pilot as well as bits and pieces of machine I'll put in a long distance call and have you back from wherever it is you're going."

"Iceland," he said.

Looking back on it, it's interesting to speculate what would have happened in the Tree Frog affair if McTeague hadn't passed the buck to me. McTeague is six feet four inches tall. I am not.

When he'd gone I thought the whole thing over and, for about the hundredth time, the idea of resigning occurred to me. Every year the cream of the universities, waving their first class degrees like banners, come and storm the bastions of independent research. Meaning not the dirty old commercial kind. Perhaps they're dazzled by the whiteness of our coats, I don't know. Doctorate theses are typed, on a variety of subjects only one in a thousand of which are of any conceivable interest to anybody at all. The frontiers of knowledge are pushed back another millimeter or two, but still they'd all be better off assembling lawn mowers; the work's more interesting.

Outside it was raining. There was a tap on the window and I opened it to admit the Institute cat, a nondescript tom who knew to a hairsbreadth how soft a touch any of us were. He was out of luck this morning, though. I clamped him firmly under one arm and took him down to Fred's room, dropping him on the lower shelf of the tea cart. He at once started to lap up half a pint of spilled boiled milk. According to Dinsdale, who goes in for psychoanalysis to a boring extent, the cat is the only member of the Institute who's remotely near being integrated, and probably Dinsdale is right.

Two

WHEN I got back to my room, Binnie was there. I'd forgotten to close the window, and she was dabbing at the sill with the end of a tablecloth. She straightened up as I came in, all grin and freckles as usual.

Binnie was a striking girl. For one thing, she had a spectacularly ugly face. Not plain; that implies a certain neutrality. Binnie's face was that of a particular type of redhead found among the Irish, the Scots and the Scandinavians; a flat-nosed, alley-cat face, all eyes and teeth, which called to mind generations of quarreling and backyard infighting. Boys with this face are always called Ginger and make you instinctively want to thump them round the ear for insolence. For a girl, a face like Binnie's could have been a disaster. The rest of her, however, was just as spectacular but for different reasons. She was exactly my height, weighed 150 pounds and swam freestyle for the West of England. She was completely good-humored and completely inaccessible. Not only McTeague but everyone else formed theories about this. I had no time for theorizing because I was too busy being crazy about her (McTeague had another set of theories about this, too). As a matter of fact the truth was very simple. Binnie made me laugh, and in my view we can do with a lot more people like that around.

"You're going to make a lot of money," I told her.

"That sounds nice," she said. "How?"

"By hammering away at about four miles of figures," I said.

"Oh. I see."

She was wearing one of her discouraging country-girl outfits, all different shades of brown and functional brogues. She took away the tablecloth and squeezed it out in the washroom farther along the corridor.

"What figures?" she asked when she came back.

"Believe it or not," I said, "this is called Flittermouse Three. It's going to be exactly the same as Flittermouse One and Flittermouse Two, only more boring because we've been through it twice already." Sometimes I think the only time staff officers in the various armed services get any real fun is when they all have to get together round some massive oak table and think up a new name for a project. As it happens, Flittermouse wasn't bad—the experiments were about various aspects of radar control at night—but even then I had a mental picture of one of the more pedantic committee members getting up and pointing out that bats don't use radar but sonar. It probably kept them arguing until teatime.

"I don't mind how boring it is," said Binnie.

"I bet you don't," I said. "It's going to mean about a hundred hours overtime."

"When are we going to start?"

"Well, not yet. I've got to go up and talk to Dr. Chapman

for a couple of days. As a matter of fact," I continued brightly, "you could come up to town when it's over and we could have a large and expensive dinner on Seeker's entertainment account. How about it?"

"It sounds marvelous."

I looked at her thoughtfully. "I suppose you haven't any idea what sort of job this is?" I asked her. "This evaluation for Chapman, I mean."

There were three girls in Statistics: Binnie, Laura, and Anne Pomeroy. Apart from being the indispensable hard core of the Institute, they formed its most efficient internal communications system, a fact which they exploited to great profit in terms of dinner invitations. This wasn't why I'd asked her to come to London, but I reasoned that she might tell me what was in Chapman's mind just the same, if she knew. But she didn't.

"All I know is that Dr. Michaelson wanted you to do it if possible."

"Me? I thought he'd given it to McTeague?"

"He wrote your name at the side of the memo when they brought it up from the office," said Binnie. "I was there."

"He didn't say anything about it when I was talking to him just now. I suppose he thought it might cost him a computer if he was nice and straightforward about it and I took it on."

"Are we getting one? A computer?"

"No," I said.

It still looked a bit odd to me. I am impatient when it comes to political maneuvering at any level. But Michaelson, I knew, saw life as a complicated postal chess game, and I could quite well imagine that if he really wanted me to go and do an evaluation for Seeker Section, his first move would be to offer it to McTeague, especially if he knew McTeague was going on holiday and would automatically try and dump the whole thing onto me. That sort of thing gives Michaelson a glow of satisfaction, and who was I to interfere with his pleasures? I went back to his office, offered to take it on as though it was all a surprise, and got neither thanks nor any information about what sort of evaluation it was.

"And please try not to be too funny when you fill in your expenses claim, Giles." Michaelson was writing an endless column of figures on the margin of a roll of used cardiograph paper. It might have been the basic equation of the universe, or his weekend shopping list in code.

"Don't worry," I told him. "The only really likable thing about Seeker is that they always pay out expenses claims without question. Even mine."

Three

The train clattered and clacked its way through various London suburbs on its way to Paddington. I sat opposite a girl whose ideas on packaging and presentation ran to preshrunk jeans and somebody's green-and-black striped football jersey, and considered Seeker and its liberal attitude towards expenses.

When I was in the R.A.F. the system had been simple. If you traveled by train, you made out a voucher. If you took your own car, you got sevenpence halfpenny a mile. In either case, you got a subsistence allowance and they didn't care if you used it to stay at the Savoy or under the pier at Brighton so long as you didn't do it in uniform. When I came out of the services and joined the Institute, things became more informal. We weren't civil servants, though we were paid on similar scales, and our normal working arrangement was that we filled in forms detailing what we actually spent. We were then, after due deliberation, repaid.

In practice this meant that if you stayed at hotels of which the Financial Committee approved, due deliberation took about a week. If you didn't, it took anywhere between a month and a year according to how little the Financial Committee thought of your habits. I stayed at the Carlton Tower and some of my expenses claims were eighteen months old and still in the machinery. But then I had independent means.

To be exact, my father had left me five thousand pounds and a Victorian brick villa in the middle of a row of identical brick villas in Prestatyn. It is possible to live on 325 pounds a year, which is the income from five thousand, but Prestatyn is cold in winter and I didn't try. On the other hand, as a supplement to senior scientific officer's pay, which was my equivalent grade, 325 pounds buys quite a lot of entertainment even after tax. I got mine by staying at the Carlton Tower and arguing with the Financial Committee, who wrote me long and polite letters on the subject.

Except when I worked for Seeker. Then, for some reason, the bills got paid promptly and without comment, (a fact which I didn't pass on to Dinsdale or McTeague). I suppose this odd circumstance ought to have rung some sort of warning bell in my mind, but it didn't.

The train hauled its way grudgingly into Paddington Station. I plodded up the slope into the sunlight of Eastbourne Terrace and crossed over to Craven Road. I like walking, and I was in no hurry.

Seeker Section headquarters are in Bayswater, which for my money is the most, if not the only, fascinating part of London. Piccadilly Circus is a roundabout dominated by a boy with a bow and arrow. Soho is an advertisement for itself. Kensington is decayed, Bloomsbury dead and the City long since embalmed and buried. Bayswater is still alive and kicking. Hard. The girls have gone off the streets and now hide discreetly behind postcard-sized advertisements in shop windows, but they're still there. Those who have a mind to can probably buy their way through to any known perversion and a few that haven't been thought of yet. Some of the mews have been pulled down and recolonized by consultant surgeons and company lawyers; their daughters study art and ride in the park.

The Russians are still there. So are the Maltese, the West Indians, the Poles, the Africans, the Bulgars, the Hungarians and the Turks. Film production units send down temporary roots in bow-fronted terraces. Companies are carved up in the expensive drinking clubs and individuals in the cheap ones. If your credit is good you can get a car, a yacht or a bazooka. For cash you can buy cocaine, marijuana, heroin, mescalin or murder.

Somewhere near the geographical center of Bayswater, three adjacent houses in one of the more disreputable terraces are occupied by Seeker. The names on the doorbells proclaim Dr. Hiram Mathison, The Planetarian Society, Wm. Beswetherick Esq., and Tempo Tours Limited. Of these, only Beswetherick exists. I pushed the bell opposite his name and waited.

Beswetherick, nominally at least, is in charge of Personnel and Requisitions at Seeker. I knew him quite well. He was a languid ex-Fleet Air Arm observer, grounded (if that's the right word to use of a Naval branch) in 1952 after the helicopter he was flying in developed rotor-bearing failure at an awkward moment. After they'd done a series of bone and skin and tendon grafts on him they invalided him out. Nobody knew how he finally gravitated to Seeker, but with Seeker that's a common state of affairs.

The electric door lock clicked and buzzed and I went in. Beswetherick's room is on the top floor and there is no elevator. When I reached the summit finally, they were all there; Beswetherick himself, Chapman, Driver and Andy Dylan. Everyone looked pleased to see me and Andy gave me a cup of coffee. I was more suspicious than ever.

Seeker—originally the Scientific Section of the Department of Special Intelligence—came into existence shortly after the end of World War II. It arose by a process of fusion and fission, appropriately enough since its first intention was to act as a clearinghouse for, specifically, atomic information. (This function is now the province of an entirely different section, Electron, which was one of the fission products of the Department as it stood in 1948).

It was merely, McTeague and I concluded long ago, that they couldn't bear to throw away all those files and had to invent someone to look after them, but nowadays Seeker's job, or so Chapman was always telling us, was to provide the answers to questions of a vaguely technical nature. Not that they ever knew the answers themselves, as Chapman pointed out, but they knew whom to ask. I was one of the people they asked, because among other things I design bits of control systems and therefore, in Seeker's view, I can tell at a glance what made any particular aircraft crash. This is something which usually requires a court of inquiry to determine, but Seeker didn't believe in committees. Also, of course, I had a security clearance up to Q-level from my R.A.F. days, which meant they didn't have to spend a lot of time and money finding out whether I was a menace to the country or not.

As a result I was continually finding myself tramping through marshes on cold, wet mornings, to view the wreckage of planes. Sometimes, for a change, they made me climb mountains to do the same thing, which I didn't mind nearly as much. I wondered which it was going to be this time. I should have realized that one day it wouldn't just be nice scientific answers they wanted.

"What we think," said Chapman, "is that they're all bits of a drone of some sort. We've got some idea of its fuselage diameter by reconstructing a few of the curved skin sections, but we can't even make a guess at its wingspan."

The glare from the dozen or so striplights in the basement ceiling was terrible until my eyes got used to it, and Driver was smoking a pipeful of seventeenth-century socks. Beswetherick had stayed upstairs, which was sensible of him.

In one corner of the cellar was a battered steel trunk full of a jumble of polythene foam. Most of the available floorspace was taken up by a huge kitchen table with about a hundred and sixty bits and pieces spread out all over it. This was the first time, I reflected, that the bits had been brought to me instead of the other way round.

Whatever it was they'd got hold of, it had come quite a cropper at some time or another. Some of the pieces were so twisted and scorched that they might have come from anything, from an aircraft carrier to a garbage can. There had been a fire, hot enough to melt not only alloy but steel plate, and a lot of the metal fragments were badly rusted.

"This is all you found?" I asked Driver.

"We didn't find them," he said.

"How did you get hold of them?"

"We bought them."

"Who from?"

If Driver had wanted me to know, he'd have told me already. He said nothing. Getting information out of Driver was like hoping for a long cool drink in the middle of the Gobi Desert, which was probably why he kept his job. He was executive head of Seeker and before that he had been a major in the Marines and before that nobody knew. He was about fifty, perhaps, but he looked old and tough and tired and as though he were always on the verge of some inward and malicious laughter. He left the science to Chapman, who was D.Sc. and thought Driver a thug.

"We wanted you to form an opinion on your own." Chapman waved a hand vaguely at the tortured sections of metal and plastic spread around the table. "Unbiased, you might say." I grunted.

"I suppose there's no doubt that they all came from the same place?" I asked.

"It had occurred to us. So far as we can tell there's no question of a plant. I take it that's what you're trying to infer."

I thought rapidly. I was sure they'd come in the trunk which now lay in the corner. Where from? Anywhere in Britain seemed unlikely or they'd have taken me there. It's difficult to form any sort of opinion about a crash without seeing the terrain around the impact point, and they'd know this perfectly well. But somebody unspecified had got hold of the bits for them. Again, how? Had he bid for them at an auction or fished them off the local rubbish dump or what? It crossed my mind that this particular trunkload of scrap metal had traveled a long way.

I picked up one of the pieces. It looked like part of a heavy rotor, machined and polished. There was a length of shaft attached to it, and shaped fluting on its under surface suggested an air turbine. It was heavy. If it was air-powered it would have taken a long time to run up to speed. Part of a gyroscope, perhaps. Next door to it on the table was a banjo union with about two inches of fine tubing trailing from each side, the ends twisted and fractured. I held this out to Chapman.

"Any fluid in this?" I asked him.

They both turned and looked at Andy Dylan, who riffled through a file of notes. Andy wore a bush jacket and K.D.s and tried hard to convey the impression that he'd just come back from some Far Eastern hellhole; Driver chewed him out at least twice a day whenever I was there. Maybe he did it even more in private, but Andy seemed not to notice, which was quite an achievement in itself. He found his place in the file.

"Sample thirty-two," he said. He picked out a photograph and compared it with the thing I was holding. I suppose, working around Driver, he'd learned to be thorough.

"Traces of, traces of, traces of . . . ah, here we are. Hydraulic fluid. Oxidized, of course." He beamed at us.

"Thank you," I said.

I put it back on the table. It was like having about a tenth of a jigsaw puzzle with most of the picture scrubbed off it and trying to guess what the whole thing looked like. Some chunks were quite straightforward. Bits of alloy skin, a wing section almost intact. There was some melted plastic sheeting which could have been fuel-tank lining. Bits of circuit board which might have been almost anything. Yards of thin tubing, no doubt all of it contaminated with hydraulic fluid (oxidized, of course), and enough valve gear of one sort and another to convince me that we were dealing with a pretty sophisticated flight control system.

I leaned across and peered into Andy Dylan's file. According to his list there were 130 items which might be identifiable and 46-odd bits of metal which probably weren't.

"All right," I said. "You really need several competent engineers. An airframe man, a propulsion unit man and an electronics man, at the very least. You know that, don't you?"

Driver nodded absentmindedly, as though he'd thought of it but it didn't matter. Chapman started to cough. We could hardly see each other across the table and I didn't blame him.

"We accept that." He recovered temporarily. "As it happens it would be impractical just at the moment."

"Dr. Chapman," I said, "let me get it quite clear what you're asking. You want me to try and evaluate this load of junk. You don't know how it fell to bits and you don't know what it was before it fell to bits. At least I hope you don't, because I hate guessing games where other people know the answers already. All right, I'll do my best for you. I'm not qualified to do so but I'll try. I shall need about four weeks and access to a good deal of scientific equipment."

I was distracted, just as I was working up a reasonable head of steam, by a noise like a woodpecker. Driver was knocking out his pipe against one of the table legs. He straightened up and put the pipe in his pocket.

"We haven't got four weeks," he said. He headed for the door and left the room. There didn't seem to be much more to say, so we all trooped out after him, leaving the light on and the door unlocked. If I'd done that at the Institute, memos would have showered down on me like confetti, but here nobody seemed to care.

There was a man in Beswetherick's office. He was about five foot six and wore a bow tie and a mauve chalk-stripe suit. When he moved closer to the window it looked more gray than mauve, but the effect was still terrible. He was going bald and he wasn't English. Even before he spoke I knew who he was. This was the man who'd sold Seeker all those bits.

"Ah," said Driver. "Very good of you, Mr. Collins. Mr. Collins, I'd like you to meet Dr. Yeoman, who gives us a hand every now and then."

Mr. Collins (I wondered what his real name was) made a small movement with his feet which suggested that he'd only recently learned not to click his heels and bow. He extended a limp and cautious hand. I shook it.

"Delighted," he said.

Driver, Chapman and Andy Dylan distributed themselves around on various chairs. Beswetherick found one for me, but I went and sat on the window sill. Outside, several floors below, three men were arguing patiently with a four[illegible] who was kicking the rear tire of a Volkswagen parked ag[illegible] the curb, and a small girl thr[illegible]w a ter[illegible]is ball relent[illegible] against an area wall.

"Mr. Collins is an engineer. His work carries him frequently to the continent, and as a result he is often able to help us." Driver nodded briskly at Collins.

Collins smiled nervously. "Excuse me, I must make plain," he said to me. "I am in tubing only. I sell steel pipes. I am perhaps hardly an engineer in the understood sense of the word."

I nodded.

"Recently," Driver went on, "Mr. Collins found himself, for reasons of business, in Hamburg. A friend of his told him that a plane had crashed nearby, and Mr. Collins was able to obtain some of the pieces for us. Those pieces you have already seen, Dr. Yeoman, and now if you would like to ask Mr. Collins any questions he will be glad to answer them for you."

I could think of about fifty right away, starting with why a pipe salesman in Hamburg should have friends who thought he was interested in crashed aircraft at all, though the answer to that was clear. I felt that Driver's account of the affair was a little short of essential detail, but there didn't seem to be any place to begin.

"Where was this? I mean, exactly where did the aircraft crash?" I asked Collins.

"In East Germany. In some trees by the Schaal See. It was very near to the border."

Outside, one of the men by the Volkswagen now had a hubcap in his hands and was turning it over and over. I tried to form a picture of the circumstances Collins and Driver had described. He had been sitting (perhaps) in a cafe in

Hamburg, and a friend had said (knowing of his interest in such things), *There's a crashed airplane forty miles east of here, would you like it? It's in the Communist Zone but I'm sure you won't mind that.* And Collins (or whatever he was called in Hamburg) had thanked his friend and got a large tin trunk, slipped over the border, filled it with as many bits of crashed airplane as he could find and then handed over the lot to Driver. It all seemed a little out of my usual field, but I was prepared to take their collective word for it, I suppose.

"Mr. Collins," I said. "How long were you at the scene of the crash?"

"Not very long. Perhaps five hours. I had a friend with me. I would have done better if I could have worked in the day, but unfortunately that was not possible, you understand."

"I see what you mean."

"I am sorry."

I looked around the room. Driver was staring at the ceiling. Chapman was writing in a small leather-bound diary. Andy was busy searching through his file. He glanced up and winked. I returned to Collins.

"I suppose you don't happen to know which way the aircraft was flying when it crashed, do you?" I asked him. "If there were trees around, some of them might have been broken by the impact, and that could give you a line."

"Excuse me?"

I started to demonstrate with my hands. "If the pieces of wreckage were here, let's say, and over here—"

"Yes of course. I know in which direction the plane was flying. It was going to the west, perhaps a little to the north. I had no compass with me."

"West. Are you sure?"

He nodded apologetically. It was an awkward fact, he could see that.

"Were there any large pieces of wreckage? I mean too large to move?"

"I do not think. But the ground is very soft, very wet, it is . . ."

"A marsh?"

"Yes, a marsh. Rather dangerous. One could sink, perhaps, and perhaps also parts of an airplane could sink."

Andy looked up from his file.

"I'm sorry, we washed those pieces you saw downstairs," he said. "In any case they were covered in . . . er . . . horse manure, before they were packed in the trunk. Bit hard to tell after that, except for obvious things like oil and hydraulic fluid and so on."

"It was a question of transport," said Collins. He looked more apologetic than ever.

I still couldn't get the picture in my mind. Collins in an East German marsh at midnight. Plodding around with a flashlight—maybe there was a moon—picking up parts of a westbound aircraft. It was near the frontier, and that meant frontier guards, Vopos. They must have heard the crash and the lakeside must have been seething with them. What had Collins done? Slipped them half a dollar and told them to come back tomorrow? Or perhaps they couldn't get near him because he was sloshing around in a quicksand, very dangerous, one could sink. I began to be glad that Mr. Collins was on our side, even if he had shifted the stuff out in a cartload of horse manure, which is what Andy seemed to be saying.

I slid off the window sill and sat down in one of the empty chairs.

"It's the bit about heading towards the west that foxes me," I said. "You really are quite sure, are you, Mr. Collins?"

But I knew he was. Chalk-stripe suit and all, he was right, and I hoped he'd charged Driver a stiff price, because he must have earned it.

"I am quite sure," he said. Andy and Chapman were both watching me. I chewed my knuckle.

"All right," I said, addressing Chapman, "let's make a working hypothesis." Out of the corner of my eye I could see that this had caused Driver to roll his eyes upwards slightly as though in pain. "Let's assume this thing was an unmanned aircraft. I further assume it isn't one of ours."

"No," said Chapman.

"You conclude that it *was* an unmanned aircraft, then, do you?" said Driver.

"I don't conclude it at all," I told him. "But it seems reasonable. Look at the list of vaguely identifiable things Dylan's got." Andy passed it over to Driver, who waved it away. "Nothing on it," I continued, "suggests any part of a manual control system. There are no bits of rudder or stick, not that that means much. There's nothing like part of a seat, nothing that could be a bit of an oxygen line, and none of the bits of skin looks as though it's meant to mate with a cockpit cover. There are no instruments, no straps, no sign of a parachute harness. We don't know if any of the bits were covered in blood. I suppose you didn't run a benzidine test on any of them before you washed them, Andy, did you?"

"Afraid not."

"All right. Never mind. Any or all of these things might have been there without Mr. Collins finding them, but let's not assume they weren't."

"Very well," said Driver. He sounded grudging, but I knew he was interested.

"Right then. Why was it heading west? That would take it over Hamburg, maybe over the top end of the Netherlands, then out over the North Sea, wouldn't it? Or is my geography all wrong?"

"Fair enough," said Driver. "If Mr. Collins is reasonably accurate, it would have passed somewhere over the north of England."

"After which there's nothing but water between it and Canada. Not that it could ever have got that far."

I went to the window again. I was starting to feel hungry. I looked at my watch and found it was half past two.

"These things are expensive," I said. "Nobody drops them in the sea just for the fun of it and I don't suppose they were doing a dry run on Fylingdales. Yes, that's another thing," I said. "Fylingdales, not to mention the rest of the stuff we've got pointing that way. Nobody in their right minds would fly a drone out into that sort of radar cover, not unless they were bomb-happy. As soon as it got out over the North Sea every Bloodhound from Margate to John O'Groats would be panicking six ways from Christmas. You could start a very nasty world war like that. It doesn't make sense."

"I agree," said Chapman.

"Perhaps it was off course," said Andy.

I looked at him. "A long way off," I said. "It ought to have been pointing in the opposite direction. But it's the only explanation."

"Not the only one," said Driver.

Andy snapped his file shut. Chapman put away his diary. Beswetherick and Collins stood up. It seemed, at last, to be lunchtime. As we all filed out into the sunshine, blinking, Driver took my arm as though he were about to divulge some profound secret.

"Three fifteen sharp," he said. "We are going up to Lincolnshire. You, me, Dr. Chapman. Shall we go in your car?"

"Yes," I said. I had no idea why we should be going to Lincolnshire, but I knew better than to ask. Anything was better than setting up the trials for Flittermouse Three, after all. I didn't know for sure if my car was ready, but Hoppy's mews garage was only five minutes' walk away and he'd had it now for a fortnight. So I let the others go to whatever pub they ate at, grabbed a sandwich at Olsens and went over to see. It looked in working order and I took it under protest, drove slowly back and picked up Driver and Dr. Chapman from the pavement outside Seeker.

Four

ROYAL AIR FORCE, Monkham Manor, is 130 miles from London, give or take a little. We made it in three hours and a bit, the long, straight East Anglian roads making up for the carbon-monoxide-laden drag out of town.

I am a good mechanic and a poor driver. All the cars I would really like to own cost above three thousand pounds, so I have evolved an approach to high speed motoring which consists of buying a cheap, strong car with a large engine and then spending another three or four hundred pounds on making it a little better. In my view, individual attention to detail is what you pay for in a car, and you don't have to pay a whole lot of import duty and purchase tax as well.

The engine of my Cresta had been stripped down and put together again rather differently by Hoppy Hobson, whose only fault is that he doesn't think cars are for driving, and has to be pried loose from them with a crowbar. Left alone, he keeps engines strapped to his dynamometer, and he'd got 180 horsepower out of mine. I was just beginning to be happy with it.

Driver slept for the whole journey, or appeared to, and Dr. Chapman showed the whites of his eyes and sometimes clutched at things in silent prayer. We got there well in time for dinner.

During the war, Royal Air Force, Monkham Manor, was a Bomber Command station. The manor house was early Victorian, decrepit even before the war and now withered beyond belief. The schoolboys who had been turned into pilots and navigators and tail gunners too early had shuttled between the officers mess in the house itself and their concrete prefabricated cubicles on the airfield perimeter, between drink and sleep, and had flown out their Lancasters whole and brought them back in pieces or sometimes not at all, and after the war the weeds took over the tarmac landing strip and the thin, cold east coast wind seeped in between the nailed slats over the hut windows.

In 1950 it was reopened, nominally as a supply depot, though the new wire fence and the guards with dogs told a different story. We stopped at the guardroom and Driver got out.

I could see him through the guardroom window displaying a batch of different colored pasteboard slips like credit cards. Eventually he found one which kept everyone happy and they let us through the mesh gates and up the drive to the mess. A civilian orderly showed us where to sleep, and a technical branch flight lieutenant took us into the bar and signed chits for our drinks. His name was Reeves, and if he knew what we'd come here for, he didn't mention it.

• • •

Bright and early the following morning—early, anyway—we were all sitting on folding wooden chairs around an unlit cast-iron stove in one of the less dilapidated Nissens.

"All" in this context meant Chapman, Driver and myself plus Flight Lieutenant Reeves, looking fresh, young and full of go, and a studious flight sergeant in heavy horn-rimmed glasses whose name was Kelsey. Reeves told me Kelsey had a Ph.D. in solid-state physic. I thought he was kidding. I went over and sat down beside Kelsey.

"My name's Yeoman," I said.

Kelsey pushed his glasses up onto his forehead to take a good look at me.

"Kelsey," he said. The glasses dropped down again onto the bridge of his nose.

"Reeves says you've got a Ph.D.," I said. "Is that true?"

"It's a little-known fact, but it's true," said Kelsey.

"Why are you here?" I asked.

He looked from side to side craftily, then leaned over toward my ear.

"For the money," he said. "What else?"

"Why aren't you commissioned?" I was genuinely curious. He stared at me.

"You're joking," he said. "I put away a thousand a year out of my pay. Ask Laughing Joe Reeves what he saves."

I remembered what they'd paid me as an acting pilot officer (N.S.A.) and saw what Kelsey meant. Even with Special Duties pay, plus what I'd occasionally and quite illegally wangled as flying pay, I'd always lost out on the deal. It was well known that the sergeants ate better than the officers.

The hut door banged open and a group captain was blown in by a small tornado. Driver and Reeves stood up. The rest of us, including Kelsey, remained seated. The group captain nodded affably at each of us in turn, clanked open the top of the stove and peered in, and hunched deeper into his greatcoat. He was a tallish, fit man with a dark mustache and a brooding air. He came across to me and we shook hands.

"Driver's put you in the picture, has he?" he asked.

"Not yet," I said.

"Tree Frog," said the group captain. "Right? My name's Nockolds, by the way. You're Dr. Yeoman, I know."

"Yes," I said. "But who or what is Tree Frog?"

"I wish to God they'd light these stoves sometimes," said Nockolds.

"They don't burn up from cold," said Kelsey, "and it's May in any case. S.S.O.s say no coke in May."

"Don't tell me how to run my station, Kel," said Nockolds, grinning at him. "Kelsey's our resident genius," he said to me.

"Or licensed clown," said Kelsey. He and Nockolds obviously had some sort of feud of long standing. The Royal Air Force is getting very democratic these days, though the Ph.D. must have had something to do with it. Nockolds turned back to me.

"Project Tree Frog," he said. "I thought a lot of the control-system work was yours anyway? Didn't you do it while you were with us on National Service?"

"I did some theoretical work on aircraft controls," I admitted. I still didn't know what it was all about.

"That's right," said Nockolds. "I forgot, you've been a civilian for the last five years or so, haven't you? So you wouldn't know. We gave most of your stuff to the people at R.A.E. when you left, and they incorporated it in a project they had on hand at the time. Now it's got back to us again and we've called it Tree Frog. It's a pilotless reconnaissance aircraft. We've got one here." He turned to Driver. "I think you might have told him some of this," he said. "I know you've got a habit of not letting your left hand know what your right is doing, but what about a bit of flexibility?"

Driver rotated the stem of his pipe where it joined the bowl. Then he pulled it out and sighted along it, squinting.

"Thought I'd leave it to you," he said. Nockolds didn't seem very surprised. He must have dealt with Driver before on several occasions at least.

"Right then," he said. "I think the easiest thing would be for us all to go over and have a shufti. Has Dr. Yeoman got a pass, or do we have to arrange that?"

"If you wouldn't mind," said Driver.

We went out into the driving wind and drizzle. Nockolds, his coat flapping, led the way past some more Nissen huts. One of them was labeled LIBRARY and another NOSE GAS UNIT. None of them looked inhabited or even in use.

We crunched along a muddy gravel path and through a small wood. The overall air of decay was stronger than ever. Eventually we arrived at a mesh fence and a low concrete blockhouse with a brown-painted steel door. Years of rain had trickled spider webs of rust down the pitted wall facing us and there was no sign of a handle on our side of the door.

To right and left the wire fencing was the only thing for miles around which was new and in good repair.

Nockolds thumped on the steel door with his palm and a second or two later it opened towards us. He stood aside as we filed in. Inside it was hot and almost pitch dark. The door thudded shut behind us and we stood around trying not to tread on each others' toes.

"This might take a little time," said Nockolds. "Perhaps you'd better all sit down."

In the event, it took twenty minutes. There were no windows, and the main source of light was the green-shaded bulb over the desk where Nockolds negotiated patiently with two sergeants. One of them was R.A.F. Police and the other Regiment, and neither of them seemed happy about letting in even Driver and Chapman, who had the appropriate passes, let alone me.

I sat on a tubular steel chair and allowed my eyes to get used to the prevailing light. I also considered Group Captain Nockolds' approach to security. Nobody in their right minds would want to run a secure establishment, military or civil. For one thing, it can't be done. I had been inside several highly restricted stations of one sort or another while I was in the Royal Air Force (the circumstances surrounding my National Service were so bizarre that it would be impossible for me to go into them thoroughly), but Monkham Manor was a new one on me. It looked as though Nockolds' idea of security was to make his restricted area look as much like a municipal rubbish dump as possible. In my view he had succeeded so well that he needn't have bothered with guards.

After five minutes he beckoned to Driver and Chapman, who went and joined the conference. I suppose they were swearing to my sobriety and reliability. Another quarter of an hour passed in silent muttering before they were all satisfied. A temporary pass was made out for me, the sergeant (Police) took my fingerprints and the sergeant (Regiment) my Institute identity card, my international driving permit and my watch, somebody pressed a switch and a door opened opposite the one we'd come in by. Beyond it was a stairwell leading down below ground level. We followed Nockolds again, myself and Kelsey leading, followed by Driver and Chapman, with Flight Lieutenant Reeves bringing up the rear. There was a faint hum of air conditioning and a smell of engine oil. The stairway descended about twenty feet into a long tunnel, which according to my rapid attempt at finding my bearings ran underground in the general direction of the airfield itself.

Despite the air conditioning, it seemed damp. Unlike the blockhouse guarding its entrance, however, the tunnel was well lit. Doors led off it at intervals. I looked into one of the doorways and saw a green leather armchair with a W.R.A.F. ops clerk in it reading a magazine. She was startled to see me, but before she could react I'd passed on.

About a hundred yards farther on the tunnel ended at a large pair of folding doors, guarded by yet another corporal policeman. He saluted, we all waved our various entry permits at him and he shoved half of the doors aside. We went in.

It was a cavern of a place, too large to be a garage, all

square cement pillars and overhead pipes with headroom clearances stenciled on them. Around the walls were the glass partition windows of engineering and maintenance bays, and in the middle, polished and gleaming, was Project Tree Frog.

Five

IT WAS a beautiful piece of machinery, and I love machines. It was also a couple of million pounds of anybody's money in terms of design and development. We fanned out in respectful silence as we approached the aircraft on its tripod (no undercarriage was visible) and walked round it.

The name TREE FROG TWO was stenciled on the after fuselage. (What happened to Tree Frog One, I wondered?) It was about twenty feet long, perhaps a shade longer, with the curious blind look of all pilotless aircraft which stems from having no cockpit.

Wingspan was, I thought, rather large for a drone. Twenty-five feet? Twenty-seven, even? There were oval pods mounted towards the tips of the wings. Auxiliary fuel tanks, I guessed.

The nose was sharply pointed and drawn out into what looked like a radio aerial. The tail ended in the polished throat of a jet tailpipe. The whole aircraft reminded me of the Australian Jindivik, except that Jindivik's air intake is high and forward, and Tree Frog Two had twin intakes back near the tail and on either side of the fuselage itself.

I crouched under one wing and ran my fingers over the smooth belly surface. I couldn't tell what the skin was. It didn't seem to be metal. I flicked it thoughtfully with my fingernails. Reconnaissance drone? I reserved judgment for the moment.

I emerged, still crouching. Nockolds and Driver were looking down at me.

"Well?" I asked.

"What do you think of her?" asked Nockolds. I don't myself, believe in calling pieces of machinery, however impressive, "her." For one thing it's inappropriate, as no doubt anyone who has tried to handle a woman as though she were a piece of machinery will be able to confirm. The essence, after all, of a well-constructed machine is that it should be predictable. For another thing, the emotions (I concede that they are emotions) which a beautiful piece of engineering arouses in me are certainly not the same as those called into play by a beautiful woman. I can understand that the crew of a bomber during a war, identifying their own lives with that of their plane, could call it by a woman's name (as a talisman, perhaps) but we weren't at war, nobody flew this aircraft and they'd chosen to call it Tree Frog in any case, so I couldn't get all worked up about it.

"Very nice," I said, using the tone of voice reserved for inspection of other peoples' vintage Bentleys.

"The control system is based on a lot of your own ideas."

"Good," I said. "Does it work?"

Kelsey, who had now come round to our side of the plane, laughed shortly. Nockolds frowned.

"What I thought," he said, "was that if you'd like to look over her, Sergeant Kelsey would tell you anything you specially want to know. We'll go over there and wait for you. Take your time."

"Over there," I saw, meant one of the maintenance bays. I could see steam wisps rising from a kettle, and Chapman and Reeves both had their tongues almost hanging out at the thought of tea. Everyone half turned to leave. Kelsey and myself seemed to be elected.

"Right," I said.

They all shot off at the double. Kelsey was looking at me in the special way Technical Branch people keep for idiotic and probably dangerous civilians. I didn't know what I was supposed to be looking at Tree Frog for, but the sooner I started the sooner we could get a clear run at the teapot ourselves. I tried to look brisk.

Kelsey climbed a set of steps and did things with screws and fasteners. In a few seconds he lifted off an upper section of the fuselage, where the cockpit canopy would have been if there had been one, and passed it down to me. It looked as though it was about a quarter of the aircraft, and it was as light as an eggshell. I put it down and he passed another piece. Then he came down himself.

"There you are," he said. "Don't break up the happy home, though, will you?"

"I'll do my best," I told him.

I climbed up myself and peered down into Tree Frog's

guts. I started at the nose, and half an hour later I finished at the tail.

If Tree Frog was what Nockolds said it was, it had some pretty odd features.

All in all, the project must have cost a fortune, whoever paid for it. For one thing, though I don't suppose I could have picked up Tree Frog with one hand, that was the general impression it gave me, and lightness costs money. A lot of the airframe was glass fiber. What wasn't glass fiber seemed to be magnesium alloy, which isn't the cheapest way to build anything.

Even so, I thought the aircraft was underpowered. I recognized the engine at once. It was the French Turbomeca Marbore VI turbojet in a shortened semimilitary version. The Marbore VI is a beautiful engine and about the lightest on the market of its type, but even in military short-life tune it only gives about 1,400 lbs. static thrust, and all the aircraft I know which fit the Marbore use two of them at once. The Jindivik has the Bristol Viper 202, which is still a small engine as they go, but it pushes out 2,500 lbs. I grant you that Jindivik has a fantastic rate of climb, but I felt that if they wanted Tree Frog to go uphill at all somebody would have to pedal hard.

What really shook me was the tankage.

"Kelsey," I said, as we walked away towards the maintenance bay, tea and biscuits, "how much fuel does that thing hold?"

"A hell of a lot. A hundred and fifty gallons inboard and

another sixty in the wing pods. As a matter of fact when she's full up and ready to go, she's more fuel than plane, weight for weight."

"Well, well," I said.

The maintenance bay looked like a bus shelter on a wet night. I cleared away a cup from the seat of a chair and sat down. Kelsey filled up the teapot, sniffed at it, decided that tea half an hour old would do terrible things to his stomach lining and mine, and started to make some more. I waited for somebody to say something.

"Nice little job, isn't she?" Nockolds started the ball rolling.

"Very impressive," I agreed. What would have happened if I'd said she was a heap of old tin? "Light, too."

Chapman cleared his throat.

"Dry weight, twelve hundred pounds," he said. "Anything else you particularly noticed?"

I began to get angry. Maybe they should have made some fresh tea for us.

"Yes," I said. "Suppose somebody tells me what all this is about? Because I'm getting a bit tired of everyone sitting around in dead silence while I try and guess what it is I'm supposed to be finding out. So far I've only been told one solid fact about that plane, and as it happens I think even that was a load of old rope."

"And what was that?" Chapman looked offended.

"Group Captain Nockolds said—back in that Nissen hut, you remember—that Tree Frog Two was a reconnaissance plane."

"Well?" said Nockolds.

"I don't believe it," I said. "For one thing that gadget out there is practically a flying kerosene tin. Fuel, fuel everywhere. Two hundred and ten gallons, according to Kelsey."

"Quite right," said Chapman.

They were all looking at me. Driver poured out a cup of Kelsey's new pot of tea, and looked expectant.

"Go on," he said.

"All right, I'll go on. Tree Frog is an expensive pilotless aircraft. With a large wingspan, which suggests it isn't meant to fly very fast, but probably very high. This is confirmed by the fact that it's powered by a lightweight, low-thrust turbojet. I suppose you carry it up and launch it from a carrier plane, so it doesn't need to climb far or fast. All right so far?"

Everybody nodded. Kelsey grinned, and I felt as though he'd awarded me a medal.

"Well," I said. "I don't know how fast the Turbomeca burns fuel, but it can't be all that thirsty. So what's Tree Frog's range? A thousand miles? More, if it doesn't have to take off and climb to altitude? That's a long, long way for a drone. In fact it makes Tree Frog look like a sort of baby Lockheed U-2, doesn't it? Only without a pilot, of course."

I was watching Nockolds closely. I knew I was home and dry.

"Tell me," he said. "Just what do you think Tree Frog is for?"

"I think you take it up underneath a bomber," I said, "and drop it off. Then it flies round in circles acting as a high-altitude target drone, while the boys down below fire rockets at it or something. Maybe you use it for high-altitude fighter interception trials. I don't know. But I'm damned sure you don't fly it five hundred miles over enemy territory and bring it back again, or even a thousand miles straight over the top."

"And what makes you so sure?"

"Oh, look," I said. "What is this? Because nobody's got enough radio-control equipment to do the job, that's why not. How much does it carry when you've put all that fuel into it?"

Chapman answered again. He seemed to be the technical facts-and-figures man.

"Two hundred pounds."

"Right," I said. "If you want me to spell it out, I will. Radio control for a hundred-mile radius or so I can believe in. If you were flying it around in the Australian desert where all the land is nice and flat and friendly, so it doesn't matter too much if you make a mistake, I'd increase the radius a bit."

Nockolds was nodding like a mandarin.

"But you're talking about a thousand-mile flight over hostile territory," I went on. "For that you need," I ticked off on my fingers, "accurate radar tracking up to a radius of five hundred miles, which you may have got but I doubt it. A sophisticated telemetry system for transmitting instrument readings from inside the aircraft, say a minimum of four navigation instruments and three fuel and engine monitors. Otherwise you may run out of gas or have the engine blow up on you. Not to mention a radio control system that's about ten times better and more sensitive than anything I've seen so far."

"There have been developments, of course," said Driver, to himself.

"Maybe. But not to that extent," I said. "Now all this, plus an autopilot, plus a whole lot of cameras to take pretty pictures of the ground, you want to weigh in at less than two hundred pounds. Well, I know they're doing marvels with transistors these days, but no. I don't believe it. Like they say, a joke's a joke, but a girl doesn't want to laugh all the time."

There was a long silence. Driver fiddled around in his coat pocket, brought out what looked like a Boys Home Workshop and started to give his pipe a decoke and valve job. After a bit Chapman fired off a small barrage of embarrassed coughs.

"I think we owe you an apology for having presented things to you in this manner," he said.

"I don't need an apology," I said. "I'll settle for an explanation."

Chapman looked across at Driver.

"Does the idea of a long-range, high-altitude drone surveillance aircraft really strike you as impossible, then?" Driver inquired.

"In the present state of knowledge, yes," I said.

"To put it bluntly, you don't believe us."

"That's about it."

"Good," said Driver. "That's what we wanted to hear. Because you will recall that we showed you a whole lot of bits of something or other from the other side yesterday, didn't we?"

I began to see. It was quite true, looking back, that a lot of the damaged pieces I'd looked at in the cellar in Bayswater might very well have come from something like Tree Frog.

"If we can't do it, neither can they. Would you agree, Dr. Yeoman?"

"Yes," I said. "I don't believe they've got all the talent and we haven't, or we'd have heard by now."

Driver smiled, full of charm all of a sudden.

"That's exactly what we thought," he said.

I didn't get anything more out of him until we were on our way back to town. Nockolds had laid on a good lunch, though I dread to think what his mess kitchens looked like if the rest of his station was anything to go by.

Chapman seemed to have decided all of a sudden that I was a fellow scientist and that I'd been shabbily treated, and spent his time being apologetic. All I wanted was to get rid of both him and Driver and take Binnie out to dinner.

I drove at between ninety and a hundred on the open stretches. Somewhere around Huntingdon, Driver came to life in the back seat. He leaned forward over my left shoulder.

"We're extremely grateful to you, my dear chap."

"You're welcome," I said. "Tell me one thing. Do you mean to say that you laid on all this pantomime just to get my opinion on the possibility or impossibility of Tree Frog as a long-range drone?"

"I'm afraid so, more or less."

"Of course you could have asked me straight out, couldn't you? But I suppose that would have been too simple. Better still, you could have asked the R and D boys at the Ministry of Aviation. Why didn't you?"

Driver was humming something from *Lohengrin*. It had obviously been a good day so far as he was concerned, but I was still annoyed.

"We wanted an unbiased view," he said. "In fact, if anything we wanted you to be biased in the wrong direction. So we told you we'd already done it. You refused to believe us. So now we know where we stand with regard," he considered his words, "with regard to anything other people may try to tell us."

"What you mean is, someone's trying to sell you the idea that all the bits in that tin trunk of yours in Bayswater come from a long-range Russian drone. Is that it?"

"Something like that has been suggested, yes," said Driver. He sounded like a politician answering a leading question.

"I thought perhaps that was it," I said. "Collins insisted it was heading in our direction when it crashed, didn't he?"

"Yes," said Chapman. "It implied, you see, that the thing could be turned round and brought back. But now I'm inclined to think it was a target drone with control failure. Of course Collins hasn't got the technical knowledge to check up on something like that, so we had to ask you."

We angled through Godmanchester and out along the road to Caxton Gibbet. I hadn't got the tire pressures right yet for high-speed work and the car was still a bit tail-happy.

"Now look," I said. "It's nice of you to put so much faith in my opinion, but I wouldn't like to be quoted where it really counted. For all I know they can fly radio-controlled planes to the South Pole and back."

"But you don't think so."

"No. I don't think so," I told him, "but that's as far as it goes."

"Good enough for the moment," said Driver. He was still cheerful. Five miles farther on he sat forward again.

"Of course you realize we can't go into the details of all this," he said. "Unless you wanted to come and work with us on a rather closer basis, that is. Purely as a temporary measure, you understand."

"No thanks," I said.

He leaned back.

"Pity."

"Look," I said. "You must have seen my Services Clearance File some time or other."

I watched him in the driving mirror. He nodded.

"Then you know I did three months technical intelligence work just before I came out, don't you? I was talked into it, and I spent half of those three months in a Spanish jail. All good clean fun and nothing to get excited about, but I prefer it where I am now," I told him. "I don't mind coming up to London once in a while to give you an opinion, but so far as I'm concerned intelligence work as a whole is about as refreshing as a quick dive into a truckload of guano. I did just enough of it to learn that. Sorry."

In the mirror I saw him smile. It was almost the first time he'd done so. We almost missed the right turn onto the B 1040, but not quite. Chapman closed his eyes.

"After all," said Driver, "you must have been pleased to see your hydraulic stuff in action. Weren't you?"

He meant the hydraulic servo-control system I'd worked

on five years ago. It had been incorporated in Tree Frog in a modified form, it's true, and I was interested to see it in practice. Roughly speaking I believe that most of the things you can do electronically you can do hydraulically rather better, at least in power control systems. None of this made me feel any more kindly towards Driver, though.

There was something nagging at the back of my mind about the whole business. I tried to pin down what it was, but I couldn't, so I drove on towards London.

Six

I LEFT the car in Kensington Gardens Square and walked round to the Prince Harold. Occasional neon street lights were glowing a dull red preparatory to turning the whole of Westbourne Grove a glaring anonymous orange. The sun was setting slowly in the west, just like it says in the script, and the air tasted of soot, sulphur and diesel fumes.

The Prince Harold was jammed tight with tiny men wearing rosettes, each determined to enjoy London life or die in the attempt. I looked around. Binnie was right over in the far corner, but her red hair picked her out at once. She saw me and waved. I did some complicated semaphore and got myself a brandy and her a gin and tonic, fought my way through the rosettes and sat down beside her.

"Thank goodness you've arrived," she said. "They're all trying to pick me up."

"It's a local custom," I explained, "and anyway I don't see what your problem is. You're bigger than most of them."

"Thank you," she said. "Had a hard day at the office?"

"Very hard indeed."

"How was the evaluation?"

"There wasn't one," I said. "They tried to sell me something, but I wasn't buying."

"So what did you do about it?"

"Blinded them with science. What else?"

"What are we going to do to celebrate?"

"Dinner," I told her. "That's what you came all the way up here for, isn't it?"

"What kind of dinner?"

"Indian, Chinese, Italian, you name it. What do you want to do with the rest of the evening?"

"Go to the pictures."

"Thank the Lord for nice normal girls," I said.

We drove back through the usual evening crowd of potential suicides to the Carlton Tower, where I paid my bill and explained why I hadn't used my room the previous night. They're used to it by now. Binnie was in peacock blue this evening and attracted a good deal of attention, as always. When she went to staff parties she still believed we all danced with her because we couldn't bear her to think she was a wallflower. Nobody could convince her of the truth, which was that when she enjoyed herself she grinned like a Cheshire cat and when she did so she poleaxed every man inside a fifty-yard radius.

We went down to East India Dock Road and ate a Chinese meal, saw an improbable spy film in which nobody let the side down, and drank some very bad champagne at a very expensive nightclub. About 2:30 A.M. London had exhausted its charms for us. We drove out through Shepherds Bush and headed west. I didn't propose to go in to work in the morning, but I knew Binnie had to. We left the street lights behind and carved our way through the fast, dark Buckinghamshire roads.

"You mustn't let them annoy you," she said.

"Who?"

"Dr. Chapman and those other people you go and see."

"I'm sorry," I said. "I didn't know it showed."

"After all they paid for our dinner. Or so you said. I've seen your expenses claims, I never came across so many lies all in one place as there are on some of them."

"You see everything, don't you?"

"A girl's got to keep her eyes open these days," she said. "Anyway, don't let them annoy you, Giles."

I could see that what she really wanted to know was what it had all been about. I wasn't going to tell her, though.

"It's just that I can't stand politics," I said. "And Chapman and Driver play politics all the time. They never let up. As far as I'm concerned a fact is a fact, but not according to them. To them a fact is just something to use in an argument if it suits you and leave out if it doesn't." I was getting steamed up again. "I'm a scientist, or supposed to be."

"What nonsense," she said. "Nobody's a scientist, not all the time anyway."

She put her head against my shoulder. I didn't think she was being objective enough for a statistician, but I didn't say so.

"By the way," she said. "Michaelson wants you to go to the Compass Committee. It's next month."

"Oh no. Not me. Not the Compass Committee."

The Compass Committee has been meeting now for about twenty years. It meets once a year as a rule, but occasionally it spawns small subcommittees. To be sent on the Compass Committee was usually reckoned to be the severest form of punishment. I wondered what I'd done this time.

"Why not?" asked Binnie. "It's in Vienna this year."

"I don't care if it's in Khatmandu," I said.

The trouble with me is that I think of my most brilliant ideas about a second too late. It happens all the time.

"Wait a moment," I said.

"I thought it might raise your morale," said Binnie.

"What would really raise my morale would be your coming along as my p.a.," I said. "That way I could even stand the Compass Committee."

"What would I do?"

"Assist me," I said.

She sat up straight and looked across at me.

"That's a proposition."

I didn't answer. I lifted my foot fractionally from the throttle, then put it down again, holding the Cresta through a bend.

"No," she said, judicially. "You're sweet, Giles, but no."

Some days you can't win. Some days you can't even force a draw.

"I'll have it carved on my tombstone," I said. The story of my life. 'You're sweet, but no.' You might at least have said, 'you're a bastard, but no.' "

"All right. You're a bastard. All men are bastards."

"How do you know?" I asked her. "Have you tried them all?"

"My mother told me."

"Oh. She tried them all?"

Somewhere, somebody blew out a tire. I heard it go. I couldn't see, I was blind, just like that. Then I realised it was the windscreen, and slammed the heel of my hand forward into the crazed-over glass. It happens sometimes. Tiny crystal beads burst around my wrist and showered in over us, but it was too late, I could feel the steering wheel dragging over in my left hand, harder, much harder than I could wrench it back, and then the nearside front wheel hit the grass and the hood slanted up, the beam from the headlight stabbing at nothing but empty sky like a searchlight, and I knew we weren't going to get back on the road, and a microsecond later that this was the time we were going to die. I slid to the right, out from behind the steering column, and pulled Binnie's head down as hard as I could into the seat cushion, and the Cresta sank down again, way down, like a tanker slapping into a choppy head-sea. Things crackled all around us and we slewed sideways and over. I don't use safety belts, and with the bit of my mind that was watching I wondered if, academically speaking, I was right. The roof leaned in on us. One of the windows burst and a piece of glass shaped like a sword slashed across and stabbed into my arm and then we were upright again for a moment before we bounced. A roll is better than a collision, there's less deceleration involved and deceleration is the killer. Then the car was rocking, upside down again now, and the sea of noise I couldn't hear died away into silence. Deliberately, I switched off the engine, though it had stopped, because the silence was punctured by a dripping and hissing of something falling onto hot metal, and it might have been petrol, or oil, or water, or blood but I didn't want to find out the hard way which it was.

I slid out from behind the wheel. I was lying on my side on the roof lining. I crawled on my belly out through the distorted gash where the windscreen had been. As I tried to squeeze out from the space under the hood I could see that Binnie wasn't dead either. I pulled her hair as hard as I could. Petrol vapor clawed its way harshly into my lungs and I wanted us both out of there. She squealed. I levered my shoulder under one of the wings and heaved. Somewhere along its length the car was pivoted on something, and it tilted. Binnie crawled out and away. I rolled out from under the wing and stood up. She was straightening her dress and blood was pouring down the side of her face and dripping onto her shoulder.

"That's the last time I drive home with you," she said. "I knew you were a menace."

"It wasn't my fault," I said. "Somebody shot at us."

"I wish you'd stop trying to push your thumb through the side of my head," she said. "It's giving me a headache."

"Sorry," I said.

I was afraid she might have cut a branch of the temporal artery, and I wasn't going to stop compressing it until I was sure. I had a short, fairly deep cut in the muscle of my left arm, but that was all. Walking away from it, they call it.

"Have you broken anything?" I asked.

"No. My dress is ruined, of course."

"I'm sorry about that," I said.

"What did you mean just now, somebody shot at us?"

"I saw the flash," I told her. But I was beginning not to believe it myself.

The motorcycle patrolman looked into the upturned wreckage of the car to make certain nobody else was left in it. He came back to us.

"Just you and the lady, was it?"

"Yes," I said.

"Lucky for you I happened by so soon. Are you sure you're both okay, then?"

"Yes, thank you," said Binnie.

"That's a nasty cut you've got. Was there any other vehicle involved?"

"No," I said.

"We've had several cars come off there," he said. "Cambered the wrong way. Were you going any speed?"

"A bit," I told him. "I think a tire blew out."

"All right then. They'll be along any minute now." He rocked the side of the car experimentally. "Write off," he said. There was no way of telling what he thought, though I could guess, and I didn't blame him.

I came back the next day. I still remembered the small flare of fire, twenty yards ahead on the offside of the road. When you've seen it once, the muzzle flash of a rifle sticks in your mind like the smell of cordite. But I was going to make sure.

I searched around. On the nearside front wheel the tire had split all the way round and half of it was looped around the stub axle. I got the wheelbrace and took the wheel itself off. There was a line of bright metal scored across the rim at one point. I took the wheel to a man in the chemistry labs. He found lead, copper and traces of nickel, so I didn't need the rest of the bullet to tell me I'd remembered right.

Seven

Two weeks later, Michaelson decided we were on speaking terms again. According to Michaelson I am a latter-day teenage hooligan undermining the foundations on which science rests. Now that I'd taken one of his staff out to a nightclub and crashed the car bringing her back home at three in the morning, his opinion was confirmed. He had pressed home his advantage by giving me ten days sick leave, (which I didn't want).

When I got to his office, it was no surprise to see Chapman with him.

We went and had lunch at the Tudor, which (as its name implies) provides at one and the same time the phoniest atmosphere and the worst food for miles around. Chapman felt quite at home and champed his way steadily through frozen prawn cocktail and frozen TV dinner divided up and dished out on several lukewarm plates instead of an all-in-one silver foil tray.

He had, he said, been asked to approach me officially on the question of temporary secondment to Seeker. He knew I was against the idea, and would not have asked me to reconsider if the matter had not been one of importance. Dr. Michaelson, my director, had agreed to let me go if I would accept the arrangement. (This didn't surprise me in the least.)

It was almost impossible, Chapman said, to find anyone with my particular combination of talents, though of course if I turned them down, they would have to do their best and hunt around. He practically broke my heart. I would be on an expense allowance, he said, sounding as though he were offering me the crown jewels.

We sat in the lounge, surrounded by copies of last year's *Illustrated London News,* and drank thimblefuls of warm wet mud. I agreed. Chapman was effusively grateful and left on the next train to town.

When he'd gone, I went round to see Binnie. She was still on her sick leave, which meant that she'd taken her calculator back to her flat and was working out other peoples' results just as she always did.

"I get so bored," she explained.

They hadn't kept her in hospital more than the mandatory forty-eight hours. I work there sometimes, giving lectures on abnormal psychology to general practitioners who see far more of it in a week than I shall ever come across in a lifetime, and Hallcroft, who normally treats me as an interfering upstart, had done a really beautiful job on the cut across her temple.

She made tea.

"How do I look?" she asked.

"Marvelous," I told her. "Before you were plain. Now you're fascinating."

"You say the nicest things."

She sat at the table and tapped away at the keys of the Halda while her tea got cold.

"Dr. Chapman was here this morning," she said.

"Was he? He wants me to go and work for them in London," I said.

"Are you going to?"

"Yes. Not that I want to, but there are one or two things I wouldn't mind finding out. So I let him talk me into it."

"What about the Compass Committee?"

"Screw the Compass Committee," I said. "McTeague is due back from Iceland any day now. Let him go to Vienna."

She pushed the calculator to the back of the table, drank her tea, and started to copy rows of figures onto squared paper. I looked over her shoulder. The figures were Dinsdale's. He seemed to be trying to correlate performance times on some rather complex task—it looked like operating variable-rate power steering, which I knew was one of his favorites—with simple reaction times. He used a sort of shotgun approach to experimental work, doing endless trials and then handing all the results over to Statistics to see if they could extract anything significant from them.

It hadn't worked this time. She added the last column of figures and then sat back.

"About that crash," she said.

"What about it?"

"You said somebody shot at us. What on earth were you talking about?"

"Forget it," I said. "It must have been shock, or something. I heard the tire blow out, it was all a bit of a nightmare. I can't really remember how we got out of the car."

I was protesting too much, and she felt it. But she didn't follow it up.

"Do I get taken out to dinner again?" she asked. "You must be going to make your fortune on expenses, or won't you get them if you go to work up there?"

"You're welcome," I told her. "This time you can drive."

I went up to London the following morning. Michaelson was so pleased to see me go that he drove me to the station himself. I took a first class ticket, bought copies of the week's car magazines from the newsstand, and spent the journey up working out what sort of car I'd replace the Cresta with. I'd been turning over an idea in my mind about getting Hoppy to work on an Armstrong Siddeley but I wasn't sure how the steering and suspension would stand up to it.

Paddington was bright and sunny, with the wind shipping up small swirls of dust on the pavements. I walked the long way round, down Sussex Gardens and along the skin-deep plaster face of Lancaster Place.

I didn't want to work for Seeker, but I'd been shot at already so I didn't seem to have very much choice.

When I rang the bell, Andy Dylan came downstairs himself to let me in. He was wearing a lime-green shirt and cavalry twill trousers to celebrate the arrival of summer.

"Welcome, cock," he said. "Tea's up."

"God bless you then, Andy my boy," I said, "for it's a friend I need and I'm far from home."

"That's a fact, mate, you are," said Andy. "But come on in anyway."

I went in.

Eight

THEY gave me a tiny office which overlooked a back garden full of coke and cats. The desk was a superannuated War Box model. The two top drawers were stuffed full of battered back numbers of Hansard, and the bottom one was empty except for a requisition slip, undated and unsigned, for five hundred rounds of ammunition, ball, 20 mm. cannon. I put this down to the air of psychological warfare which surrounded Seeker in general and Driver in particular.

At half past twelve I went down to Driver's office on the ground floor. It was the first room I'd seen in the building which looked even remotely businesslike. There were Chubb locks at the top and bottom of the door, for one thing, and about a quarter of one wall was taken up by the door of a safe. The windows were double glazed and the blue carpet looked too good to be on anybody's inventory.

Andy followed me in and shut the door. Driver was in front of the fireplace. Behind his desk sat a man I'd never seen before, eating an orange with great care and precision.

Driver performed introductions. Andy disappeared through a doorway at the far side of the room, and came back a moment later with the inevitable files.

"Glad to see you're none the worse for your accident," said Driver. "How is Miss Abrams?"

"She's fine," I said.

Sloane—the man behind the desk—looked up from his orange. He was older than Driver, with that air of careful preservation which comes from years of working in the service of H.M.G., and he had bright button eyes. I didn't like him.

"Was it an accident?" he asked. His voice was precise, unmodulated. The B.B.C. would have loved it.

"What else could it have been?"

"We understood that you had been conducting some sort of forensic inquiry of your own," said Sloane. "After all, you removed the wheel. Why did you do that?"

"All right," I said. "I took it off because I thought the tire had been punctured by a bullet. I wanted to find out if it had, or if I was being bloody silly."

"And what did you find out?"

"I found the mark where the bullet struck the wheel rim."

"Why didn't you tell anyone about this?"

Sloane finished the orange. He took out a handkerchief and wiped his fingers, though they hardly needed it.

"Such as who?"

"Us. Or the police. You didn't tell them at the time of the accident, or later, so we gather. Why not?"

I sat down. Driver was a leather armchair man when it came to office furnishing, or maybe he lived here too. It was quite possible.

"Listen," I said. "We can get all this straightened out just so long as one thing is clearly understood by everybody. Information is a two-way traffic. At the moment you've got it all and there doesn't seem to be any left over for me. Mr. Dylan has got my Services Clearance File over there, so you know who I am and what size shoes I take. I've given you my opinion on Tree Frog, which you have undoubtedly added to some other file. All I've been given is a load of old codswallop about that plane up in Lincolnshire. Now if you think that this is where I stand to attention and you ask all the questions, you'd better all take a deep breath and think again. Then you can start by telling me who you are," I said to Sloane, "so that I can open a file of my own."

Sloane looked like a man who'd forgotten to look in his boots for scorpions that morning.

"I am in Defense Intelligence Six. I don't suppose, Dr. Yeoman, that means very much to you, but you are welcome to the information."

"Thank you," I said. "You're right, it doesn't, but it's a start."

It should have meant a great deal to me, of course, but as I said, I hadn't done my homework.

"Intelligence, in nearly every country in the world, divides itself naturally into two opposing factions, though I don't suppose they'd admit to any opposition. There is Defensive Intelligence and Active Intelligence. Roughly speaking, Defensive Intelligence is concerned with exposing other peoples' intelligence networks, and active intelligence with setting up one's own. In the U. S., for instance, the defensive arm is the F.B.I. and the active arm the C.I.A. In Russia, the corresponding arms are the KGB and the GRU; in West Germany, the Office For Protection of the Constitution and the Gehlen Organization; in France, the Ministry of the Interior and S.D.E.C.E. In Britain, M.I.5 (now D.I.5) is the defensive, and Defense Intelligence Six the active branch.

None of this takes into account the fact that all the armed forces in each country have their own intelligence units, both centrally coordinated (America's D.I.A.) and individual (our Special Investigation Branches and D.N.I.), not to mention the Special Branch, Scotland Yard. Milling around somewhere in the middle of all this are organizations like Seeker, Peeper, Electron, and Shooting Star in Britain, and S2, S3, State Department Intelligence, the Directorate of Intelligence, and the Atomic Energy Commission in America.

None of this was clear to me then and in fact it still isn't, but the salient fact which I ought to have picked out, but didn't, was that Sloane was from D.I.6, not D.I.5. As it was, he was quite right. He could just as well have said he was from the little green men in Mars for all the difference it made to me.

Sloane went off to lunch. Andy Dylan marched me up to Personnel, where Beswetherick, languid as ever, took my Clearance File and riffled through it.

"I see you write poetry," he said.

"That's right," I agreed. "I also prefer plain to milk chocolate."

"We'll bear it in mind." He turned over one or two pages. I got the impression he knew it by heart anyway. "It also says here," he went on, "that you have six hundred hours flying time, mainly as observer. That's the figure from your log. And that, officially and unofficially, you have flown as pilot in the following aircraft: Dove, Anson, Dakota, Magister, Comanche, Chipmunk, but you have no civil license. On the other hand you have got Crew Rating, Parachute, in both Jump and Ejection. Are all these facts reasonably correct?"

"Yes."

"Good." Beswetherick ticked busily against them. "It's just that there might be some question later on of your flying in the launch aircraft on a drone run. I want to know whether to put you in as passenger or crew if it should arise."

When I'd been doing trials work at Farmborough (this was at the time when we had a spate of strapping pilots into complicated physiological recording rigs while they were flying, I forget for what exact reason) there was a ruling about Passengers and Crew. I remember the first pilot who took me up explaining it to me. "If you've passed out on parachute," he said, "you're crew. If not, you're a passenger. If you're a passenger and the plane catches fire, I have to make sure you're all right before I get out myself. If you're crew, I shall just yell 'out' and if you say 'what?' you'll be talking to yourself." In practice, of course, this meant that you were a lot more likely to get permission to fly if you'd passed out as crew, so I did, just the same as everybody else.

Maybe something of the sort applied now, I thought. Beswetherick was adding details of the number and state of repair of my teeth to a Hollerith card. I wondered if he was transferring me, so far as Seeker was concerned, from Passenger to Crew.

"Indemnity waiver, sign here please," said Mrs. Maitland. "And this is your inventory, sign down there at the bottom please, and here's your duplicate. Thank you." She was the only person in the building so far to have a nameplate on her door: MRS. E. P. MAITLAND, ADMINISTRATION.

Andy was still acting as general factotum and interoffice messenger. The lime-green shirt was starting to stick to his back in patches. I realized I knew very little about Andy, though on my previous visits to Seeker I must have seen him oftener than anyone else.

He had an office next door to Chapman, but he never seemed to go there; he signed letters, but he had no apparent authority. He must have reached voting age, but you couldn't tell by looking at him.

In the end I decided that all government departments had trainees and there was no reason to suppose that Intelligence was any different. As it happens I was quite wrong, but meanwhile he was the only person around who spoke my language and I was glad he'd decided, or been told, to follow me around.

For a moment, I thought Mrs. Maitland was going to hope I'd be happy here, but she didn't say anything. She asked if there was anything I wanted and I said yes, I'd like to get rid of all those copies of Hansard. She promised to do something about it, told me what I could leave in my room and what had to be kept in Driver's safe, and that was that.

"What did happen to Tree Frog One?" I asked.

"Bit hard to say," said Driver. "It's at the bottom of the sea somewhere. About fifty miles west of Lundy Island, as near as we tracked it."

Driver's office, with the blinds down, looked and felt like a mission-briefing room. Andy was manipulating a slide projector. Driver slumped, half-hidden, in one of the leather armchairs, and Sloane, unseen and unheard, was hiding somewhere in the rim of shadow around the central cone of light where I sat wishing I had something to take notes on.

"Receiver failure, they thought." Andy's voice sounded out of the gloom. We had been there about four hours, and at last I felt I was starting to find things out about Tree Frog.

"What it amounts to, then," I said, "is that you've got an efficient research vehicle in which you can run trials of various types of radio command gear, but nobody's come up with a long-range control system which really works."

"Not yet," said Driver. "Mind you, it's just a question of time, all these things are. And of course when they do get the bugs out of the electronic side of things, Tree Frog itself will switch from research to operational surveillance."

This seemed reasonable. I was still trying to decide how much of what they were telling me was the truth and how much was more old flannel, but I cast my mind back to Royal Air Force, Monkham Manor and Nockolds' underground garage. A lot of time and money had gone into the airframe of Tree Frog. The fact that Driver now said it was a research plane squared with other things I'd noticed about it, such as the large empty space amidships, far larger than one would have expected in a well-designed operational drone, where space is at a premium. But if they were still testing various configurations of radio control gear, then it made sense. It gave room to work and room to fit in assembly lash-ups.

"How long is it going to take the electronics boys?" I asked.

"That's difficult," said Driver. "You can never get a straight answer out of Research and Development."

"I know," I said.

"They're talking about two years from now, assuming a radio-radar control system with a range of seven hundred miles."

I still didn't see, in that case, what all the immediate rush was about, but I let it go.

"Thank you very much," I told them. "That's enough to be going on with as far as I'm concerned."

"Splendid," said Driver. "In that case, we can get on with the more complicated side of the picture."

I was beginning to flag, but the others were as brisk as ever. Coffee had come and gone. I looked at my watch and saw it was half past eight, so we were all on overtime.

Andy pulled the slide carrier across again and yet another picture of a satellite flashed up on the screen.

"See-See Four," said Driver. "We reckon that the Americans are putting up about one new surveillance satellite every fifteen days or so. All very well as far as it goes, but of course it's expensive. And orbital jobs have their disadvantages."

"Such as the fact that everyone knows when and where they're coming round again," I suggested. "So it's pretty easy to keep out of sight."

"Yes."

"The U-2 was a better bet."

"In that respect, yes. Of course the Russians had U-2 sorted out way back in 1957 or so, but they didn't have anything that could fly that high, so there was nothing much they could do except throw handfuls of gravel at it until the Powers flight in 1960. Then they were able to go to town on it, show trial, the lot."

"So now," I said, "everybody has decided that pilotless planes will be much less embarrassing all around? Nobody to interrogate if things go wrong. Nobody to put on trial, and the rest of us can't be expected to get into a lather about bits and pieces like Collins sold you. Is that it?"

"Yes," said Driver. "That's about it."

"And you, or I suppose I ought to say 'we' now, are engaged in a little private bit of the secret war to see who can get one into operational trim first?"

"Yes."

I thought it over. "It sounds a bit academic to me, but I can believe you," I said.

There was a slight rustle from the back of the room. I had forgotten all about Sloane. He had said nothing, made no sound, for the last five hours. He came forward now into the light, blinking once or twice.

"I'm afraid the matter is rather more than academic," he

said, "and I propose to explain to you why, if you will bear with me. Tree Frog, as of course you've noticed, is made largely of fiber glass and alloy. This means that the plane as a whole has a very low radar echo for its size. In fact, in order to track it at all during flight trials, with our present equipment, we've had to fit traveling-wave reflection amplifiers under the wings.

"If we assume, as we must do, that our opponents are working along the same lines, then whoever gets one into the air as a going concern is going to cause the other side a lot of expensive headaches." He tapped the arm of my chair. "To put it bluntly, somebody is going to have to get a whole new radar program under way, just to look for these things. I don't know if you'd care to hazard a guess what that sort of program would cost."

I could see what he meant. How do you track twenty feet of fiber-glass plane at sixty thousand feet? You can bounce microwaves off it, sure, but you can bounce them off crows, too, and little bits of freak weather, and flying saucers if you're the sort of person who looks for them.

If what Collins had brought in from his midnight jaunt into East Germany was a fully, or even halfway, operational Russian equivalent of Tree Frog, then not only would we have to start building bigger and better radar sets (and bigger and better ways of sorting out fiber-glass drones from crows) but it would all have to be done in a hurry.

Crash development programs, it is well known, cost about three times more than normal ones.

What it meant in the end was that the table stakes in this particular poker game added up to about twenty million pounds. Not to mention questions in the House. I thought of the trunk full of little bits and pieces in the cellar below us, and the Cresta rolling over and over down a bank with a bullet-ripped tire. Then I thought of Binnie with the long cut across her forehead pouring a curtain of blood, and I didn't like any of it, but it looked as though I was stuck with it.

"What happens now?" I asked.

There was very little to it. What they wanted me to do, they said, was to attend the Compass Committee meeting in Vienna. I had already arranged to do that, they understood.

If, while I was there, anyone looked as though they wanted to have a casual chat about developments in long-range, high-altitude reconnaissance drones, it would be nice (said Sloane) if I could convey the impression that we were all set to put one into the air right now. And that was all.

"Of course," said Driver, "we don't want you to walk about the place in a T-shirt with Tree Frog on the front and GO GO GO on the back. But after all you'll be at an aviation conference, and there'll be plenty of your colleagues about the place from various countries. What we'd like is for a vague impression to filter through to other people that they'd better start thinking about large research appropriations for radar defense. You see?"

I told him I saw. Just what somebody was trying to convey to us with all those bits of rubbish Collins collected, I said.

"Quite right," said Driver. "Fortunately we were able to call upon your expert knowledge, weren't we, so it didn't quite come off. Well, now we'll bloody well put the fear of God into them, and it would be nice if you could just, shall we say, sow the seed. If you follow me."

"With a show of reluctance?"

"That's the ticket," he said. "A show of reluctance. I couldn't have put it better myself."

Sixty hours later I was clattering down the steps from a Trident at Schwechat Airport in watery sunshine and a Force Seven gale. The wind whipped minuscule waves across the pools of rain dotting the tarmac, and we politely upstaged each other all the way over to the bus for the Sudtirolerplatz.

Nine

EARLY next morning the wind had dropped and the sun was shining as though it was trying, for a change. I left my hotel room and walked along the canal.

There was a time when I'd thought of going to Vienna University to study medicine, but nothing came of it. A pity, because I'm prejudiced right from the start in favor of people who can call one of their streets the Jasomirgottstrasse, and I like baroque.

Vienna, city of the baroque, is what the guide books say, and they're right. Leave out the Karlskirche and the Piaristenkirche and the Museum, forget all about the architecture, and it's still true. Baroque cream cakes. Mozart, all the Strausses, the Staatsoper, the Spanish Riding School. What about the great baroque schools of psychology erected by Freud and Adler? Perhaps it's something in the air.

Steam drifted about the surface of the water, spilling over the gunwales of boats. I had forgotten about Seeker. I reflected that the Compass Committee itself was baroque in conception, if it came to that. I am not a committee man myself, except when forced into it. I have attended brisk, rectangular, ice-water committees run by Americans, whispered committees in Whitehall, and those Ministry of Supply Committees in Aldershot which are the most frightful of all.

No committee achieves very much (except perhaps in Russia, and even then I doubt it), but the Compass Committee never achieved anything at all. It was supposed to redesign aircraft instruments, having absorbed, during the course of its long and uneventful life, the Altimeter Committee and the Attitude Indicator Research Group, but of course it did nothing of the kind. Nor would it do so on this occasion, I knew.

I turned right, up the Rotenturm Strasse, and arrived at the committee rooms at two minutes past nine.

I found I was sitting between Holmqvist from Sweden and Captain Yancy Brightwell of the U. S. Air Force. I knew both of them, since only erosion and gradual replacement alters the membership of the Compass Committee.

"Long time," said Yancy.

"A year," I said. "How are things?"

"Fine. We've got a knockout this year. You wait and see."

It was early summer and the first heat wave had just started. All the radiators were on, and Professor Giacometti, the chairman for the session, fought a three-day losing battle with the air conditioning. It had been installed, I supposed, as a gesture of welcome to Yancy. As it happened he liked open windows as much as the rest of us, but it would have taken a special subcommittee to get them opened, so they stayed shut.

By the end of the first morning it had been established

that, as usual, only the Americans had any sensible proposals. Yancy produced his knockout, which consisted of a vast folder like an ad agency's campaign presentation, all arrowed diagrams and diachromes. He went through it in detail. It was clear to me that his ideas were workable, could be grafted onto existing aircraft systems without too much modification, and were backed by capable and thorough research. I sat back, because I knew he'd never get the scheme past Giacometti, let alone Royce of the Professional Pilots' Association. He knew it too.

I remembered why I was supposed to be here.

Who was going to back me into a corner and start asking me casual questions about Tree Frog, and when?

There were three new faces at the table this year, and I checked my seating plan to find out whom they belonged to. Pzenica, from Poland. Neilson and Kiess, from Switzerland. The two Swiss I knew nothing about. Pzenica had written a paper on radar defense the year before, which I'd translated, but I'd never met him. The Poles have a streak of divine madness which can sometimes lead them to break up a whole meeting if they're in form, so I was glad to see him.

Yancy ran through the last of his diagrams and we broke for lunch.

"Another day, another dollar," he said. "Let's grab a couple of beers, shall we?"

We went out and crossed the Ring into the Stad Park. I got on well with Yancy because he had a fairly cynical approach to applied research himself, which is unusual in the States where they take it, as a whole, even more seriously than we do. He told me about his wife and the new baby they'd just had. Then we moved on to his aircraft instrument ideas.

"You going to back us?" he asked.

"I doubt it," I told him. He didn't seem very put out.

"Oh well," he said. "*C'est la vie.* You get me the next one, though."

We drank another beer, watching the students in polite and decorous couples.

"You hear anything about a broken-up Red recce plane, Giles?" he said.

I bounced my attention back to him.

There is an old joke about security in the R.A.F. Security means first of all not telling the Navy. Then not telling the Americans. Then not telling the Russians, only that doesn't matter so much. But in any case I didn't want to get all tangled up with Yancy over this business because he was a friend, even if he was conceivably a Russian spy, which I thought unlikely.

"What plane is this?" I said.

"Nothing much," said Yancy. "Just a friend in Hamburg a couple of months back told me. Apparently there was some sort of expedition across the fence into the East, big hoo-ha, you know? Some bright boy knocking off a crashed plane, that was how the story got back to me. I deal with these things as a sideline, you know, only there was nothing but a whole lot of silence from then on. I wondered if you'd heard about it, that's all."

"Not me," I said. "It's not in my line anyway."

"Okay," said Yancy peaceably. "Only you used to be in the trade, I recall."

"For three months," I said.

"Oh. Never again, eh?"

"That's right," I told him. We walked back to the afternoon session in the hothouse.

When we got into the lobby, the first thing I saw was the back view of a redhead getting into the lift. I couldn't believe it was Binnie, but it was.

"What the hell are you doing here?" I asked.

"Don't sound so welcoming," said Binnie. "Dr. Michaelson sent me over. He's got some paperwork for you. He wanted me out of the way until my face got better, too, I think."

I introduced her to Yancy, who looked a little nervous. The scarline across her temple was healing nicely but it was still red and angry, and she looked more than ever like an alley cat after a tear-up fight.

"Is that all?" I asked her. "There's a very good postal service, so they tell me, and you could have gone to the South of France."

"What's the matter with you?" she said. She turned to Yancy. "Three weeks ago he *wanted* me to come over here as his p.a., and now all of a sudden he doesn't."

"He's got no finer feelings," said Yancy.

"Is that what you are?" I asked her. "My p.a.?"

"That's right," she said. "Only don't get any bright ideas. I'm supposed to take notes, that's all."

The truth was that I wasn't all that pleased to see her here. In other circumstances I'd have been overjoyed, but I didn't like the idea of passing on casual secret information to whoever might be in the market for it with Binnie looking over my shoulder. She'd want to know what went on. She's quicker off the mark than most.

Just the same, it was nice to see her. I decided to relax.

The Compass Committee ground on through its second and third days. Everybody said predictable things, and then repeated themselves.

Our own position was the same as always. That was confirmed by the letter Michaelson had sent me, which in turn was a summary of official government mood and opinion. Reading the bits between the lines as well as the text, it came out as the usual stone-walling. We didn't like the existing compass and we hated the existing altimeter. We hadn't developed any ideas for replacing them because we hadn't been given any money to do so. We liked the U. S. system (Yancy's), but we were still annoyed with them over the Decca Navigator affair, so we weren't going to say so.

At five o'clock on Thursday, Professor Giacometti declared the session closed and invited us all, as guests of the Italian Government, to cocktails at the Konigstuhl Hotel.

And that seemed to be that.

Ten

THE reception room at the Konigstuhl was distilled essence of Palm Court filtered through matchwood abstracts. The best of the old and the worst of the new. Professor Giacometti beamed paternally at all of us, expressed his pleasure at the fact that we'd achieved something during the present session and got no disclaimers in reply. There was a string quartet. Yancy Brightwell, Holmqvist and myself drank bourbon because the scotch seemed to be Japanese, and Binnie drank Asti Spumante because she liked it better than champagne. Giacometti cornered her to discuss the matter with her. Yancy watched them, in bursts, over his shoulder.

"Don't mind if I say this, will you, Giles?" he said. "But taking a considered view, she's what I'd call a real homely girl, isn't she? Nice, though. Don't get me wrong."

"I know what you mean," I said.

"She is not a beauty, certainly," said Holmqvist judicially. "But . . ." He stopped.

"I know what *you* mean, too," I said.

"How'd she get that cut on her head?" asked Yancy.

"We were in a car smash," I told him.

"Oh." He seemed to think this was a good enough explanation. Binnie turned round, saw us all looking in her direction, and waved. Then she went back to Professor Giacometti. I wondered what subject they'd got onto now.

"Sensible idea, though," said Yancy. "What I mean is, you don't necessarily want distraction on one of these seminars, do you? What you need is a competent assistant, and I'll bet she's that. And no temptation to step out of line, is what I mean."

"That's all you know," I said.

At half past seven Binnie detached herself from a small group which now included the two Swiss and Royce as well as Giacometti, and came over to us.

"Having fun?" I asked her.

"Of course I am. But I'm afraid I'll have to go. I've got a plane to catch."

"That seems a pity."

"I know. But I've already booked my return flight."

"Why not cancel?" I said. "You can always get on another one."

"If I were you I'd run for the one you're on now," said Yancy. "Giles here has got designs on you, did you know that?"

"I can hardly believe it," said Binnie. "But I think you're right, as it happens. About the flight, I mean."

"I'll drive you to the airport," said Yancy.

When they'd gone I got myself another drink and sat down in a tub-shaped chintz armchair. The string quartet was still going great guns, but the party seemed to have thinned out a bit. Someone I didn't know came over and suggested I join a party going to the theatre that evening, but I didn't feel like it. I'd been quite right. Having Binnie around made even the Compass Committee quite bearable, and now that she'd gone I felt bored.

What was I going to tell Driver when I got back? That the only person who'd shown any interest in reconnaissance planes was Yancy Brightwell? I didn't see that getting information, true or false, across the Atlantic and into the State Department was a process that needed any help from me. No doubt Seeker had a file on Yancy. They probably had one on Yogi Bear, but I wasn't going to help them fill up their files.

I looked up. Pzenica, the radar man from Poland, was standing over me. He had one of the Swiss with him. Both of them held glasses of vodka. "Kiess," said Pzenica, waving at his companion. I'd seen the bottle on my way to collect myself another bourbon. It was the Warsaw State Monopoly stuff, 140 proof and probably explosive. Kiess was a short stocky man with dark hair, and he had a slightly glassed-over look, inevitable when drinking with the Poles.

"You are Dr. Yeoman?"

Pzenica extended his hand, I fought my way out of the billows of chintz and shook it. He was a little taller than I was, and he'd evidently heard all about how we in the West judge a man's character by his handgrip, or else he practiced karate and didn't know when to lay off.

I told him yes, I was. Kiess inclined his head slightly, with great care. His mind seemed to be very far away.

"Everyone else is very very tired," said Pzenica briskly,

looking round the room, "or else they wish culture. We do not, nor do you, I think. I have a great many English friends and they are all great drinkers."

Perhaps he had us confused with the Irish? He was quite positive about it.

"I hope you will join us? Dr. Kiess is in flying medicine, is that what you call it? I have many friends in Vienna too, they will welcome us."

"Fine," I said. It seemed to be the only thing to do. Maybe they wanted to talk about Tree Frog, but in any case I could hardly let down the British reputation for drunken jollity.

We went to a cellar somewhere on the other side of the canal, and then to another. Pzenica's friends welcomed us everywhere we went. Maybe he spent all his time here at conferences, or maybe he just made friends easily. We drank and listened to someone playing a guitar. Nobody talked about long-range reconnaissance aircraft.

Some time around midnight we fought our way through thick salt beef sandwiches. Kiess had lost his glazed look and seemed withdrawn and disapproving, and I guessed he was within an inch of sliding under the table. We had acquired two more of Pzenica's friends, a dentist called Maier and a tall, thin man who looked like a lizard and kept muttering things about Koestler.

Pzenica leaned across me and shook Kiess by the shoulder. "Otto," he said.

"Yes," said Kiess.

"We shall go now. To the party. All right?"

"Yes," said Kiess.

"You too," said Pzenica to me.

"All right," I told him. It had been a year or more since I'd done this sort of thing and I was beginning to feel out of practice.

"Good. You will like it, they are friends of mine," said Pzenica. "It will be extremely cultural."

"I thought you said you didn't like culture," I said.

"Did I say that?" He seemed surprised. "Anyway, we go now."

We climbed up into the warm night and went.

All cities have their troglodytes. Perhaps those cities which have been under occupation within memory have a larger share than others. Perhaps not. In the cities of Middle Europe there exists that most nebulous group of cave dwellers, with nothing in common except memories; the displaced and dissected aristocracy of the old world.

I didn't know who our hosts were, and Pzenica didn't tell me. It didn't surprise me to hear him addressed as 'Count.' He could have been anything, a con man or a king. The fact that he'd written a research paper on radar meant nothing; it was his brain which kept him afloat in the world, not his ancestry.

We sat at varnished pine tables, on chairs which were old when Mohammed IV, the King of All Earthly And Heavenly Kings, brought his million-strong army to threaten the Emperor Leopold and took it away again empty-handed.

It was impossible to see who was to right or to left of us. Each table had a candle, and if you moved your hand away from the table edge it was in darkness. Kiess seemed to be asleep. Maier leaned back against the rough plaster wall.

The lizard had disappeared somewhere on the journey over here. Pzenica drank steadily, sometimes looking into the blackness and appearing to recognize someone with a flick of his hand.

Out of vision, jazz was being played on a spinet. I couldn't tell if it was live or recorded, nor where we were, nor even if we were above ground or below. Six feet away I could make out the faint shape of an arch. After a length of time I couldn't even begin to guess at, the beam of a spotlight burned a tunnel down through the smoke and threw a circle of light on the curtained mouth of the arch. Then the heavy tapestry lifted aside and the girl stepped through.

Pzenica had said it would be very cultural, and he was right. This wasn't girlie-in-a-cake stuff, it was strictly for the grown-ups. She hadn't made the mistake of starting with anything on. It is possible for a woman to remove her brassiere gracefully, even delicately, I concede. But no girl can take her panties off in public, out of context, and pretend that it's an art form, though it's a common error.

She came forward into the light. She was naked, and the tips of her breasts had been silvered. She must have stepped straight from a bath of oil, for she not only glistened and streamed with it, but droplets fell from the lobes of her ears and her fingers and pooled on the stone floor at her feet. She was about five feet six, square-shouldered, a country beauty rather than a city girl, and her black hair slicked back behind her head and neck and stuck to her shoulders. Her eyes were half closed and she moved very quietly to the sound of the spinet, in a confined arc and never more than a few feet from the archway. She raised her hands and grasped the shining rope of her hair and shook it, and when she let go it slapped downward in two oil-wet strands onto the steep upper slopes of her breasts. She trod the edge of her stage as though sleep-walking. There was no sound except the ageless, parchment tone of the spinet and the small sounds of her bare feet on the stone. If anything was ever beautiful, it was this. When she reached the table where we sat, quite suddenly she flicked her eyes open, looking towards Pzenica. Then she smiled and leaned quickly forward and snapped at the smoking wick of the candle with her fingertips. There was an oily splutter and it went out, and she laughed very quietly and stepped back into the bluish disc of the spotlight. I could see, now that she was close, the twin hairline incisions at the base of her breasts where she'd had the plastic inserts put in which held them high and firm. I remembered that Vienna was also famous for cosmetic surgery and thought that this, too, was part of the concept of baroque, to mold and alter living flesh to conform with the marble and plaster perfection of the statuary outside in the parks and squares.

Then she was gone. The oil which soaked her was gently scented with lemon, and that and the slight stirring of the tapestry curtain were the only things that recalled her presence. I felt the backs of my hands. I thought I was being detached, but they were running with sweat. Someone filled my glass, and Pzenica lit the candle again. He held it over towards Kiess and Maier. Incredibly, they both looked asleep. "She sometimes has that effect on men," said Pzenica, and laughed. I felt wide awake myself.

"Well," said Pzenica. "What now?"

"I hadn't really thought," I said.

"Would you like to talk to True?"

"Who?"

"The girl who has just danced for us. Are you interested in her?"

"I'm interested all right," I told him. "But I don't think my constitution will stand it right now."

"Ah, your constitution," said Pzenica. "She will not bite you. Come with me."

He got up from the table. It was still almost pitch dark, and he must have drunk at least a quart of nearly absolute alcohol over the course of the night, but he still seemed as steady as a rock. I got to my feet too, perhaps a shade less steadily. I could hardly refuse his invitation, not that he seemed for a second to consider that I might. I felt the national reputation might be called in question in other directions if I hesitated. Also, I didn't want to.

There seemed to be about four miles of corridors, all of them black as night and full of corners. Pzenica went ahead, humming some ancient Polish melody.

Light showed faintly in a doorway. He stopped. "True?" he asked. There didn't seem to be any reply, but he pushed open the door and went in. I followed. I can only claim that I would never have done so if it hadn't been about four o'clock in the morning and if I'd been sober.

Also, somebody had poured me a drink with a bit more zip to it than usual, I began to realize.

There is no such thing as the little pill you slip into someone's scotch and then wait until, five seconds later, they keel over unconscious. If there were, hospital anaesthetists would be using it all the time. But there are several things which can start to catch up with you after five minutes or so, especially after a ten-hour drinking session, and even more especially if you aren't too critical about what your drink tastes of.

I could see Pzenica's face hovering in front of me. It looked about the size of a house. It had an incredibly smug expression on it and I wanted to hit it, but I couldn't move very well.

"Curiosity killed the cat," said Pzenica. At least I think he said it. It might have been me.

Eleven

CONSCIOUSNESS seeped in on me, an image at a time.

My clothes were wringing wet, my mouth was dry. Dehydration. I unstuck my tongue from the floor of my mouth and at once the acrid taste of chloral burst through. Old-fashioned, chloral hydrate, crude, but effective if there's enough of it. The original Mickey Finn is chloral in alcohol. I felt terrible.

Soggy leather straps were flailing around inside my skull. I hoped I wasn't going to be sick, because I seemed to be in some kind of a box. Like Collins' bits of airplane. A tin box. Tin trunks seemed to be figuring prominently in whatever it was I was supposed to be doing. But what about the rumbling noise?

Then I smelt petrol. For a second I fought with part of me that was certain I was still upside down in the Cresta after the crash. I swung my hand up and hit it on metal at once.

The clockwork motor at the back of my brain put all the pieces together and came up with the answer that I was in the trunk of a car, a big car, an American car. It was pitch dark and I could hear the tires hiss beneath me like rain on a wet pavement.

My eyeballs tried to crawl back into their dried-up sockets like hermit crabs. It was the hangover of all time, and I decided to roll over and go back to sleep and let things sort themselves out without me.

Self-preservation dragged me back awake about twenty seconds, or hours, later. I moved over onto my back and tried to orientate myself. There was lots of space and I hadn't been tied up. We were traveling fast and there didn't seem to be much I could usefully do, but I tried to concentrate. I was being taken somewhere. They say you never have a better chance of getting out than you do *before* they get you there, wherever it is. The trouble was, I didn't know how long I'd been out, so I couldn't tell how far we'd traveled already. Nevertheless.

I felt around. The trunk was empty except for the spare wheel which was somewhere over to my right. There was room for both of us, but what I wanted was a tire lever, a jack handle. I was out of luck.

My left hand brushed against a bunch of wires running along the side of the trunk to the rear lights. How about that for a start? Rip out the wiring to the lights and some nice policeman will stop the car and I can bang on the lid and scream blue murder.

Go one better. Pull wires loose. I did so. Feel in pockets. Not a dicky bird, oh yes, wait a moment, there was a penny. Excellent. Scrape a patch of metal bare, anywhere, nice shiny bare metal. Grab the ends of the wires and grind them down onto the bare patch, hoping the trunk isn't full of petrol fumes or it'll be like inside a five-hundred-pound bomb when the fuse goes pop. Sparks crackled and spat. The wire ends went dead, with luck that'll have blown a fuse or two, maybe even put the headlights out.

Nothing happened for about a minute, then the car braked slowly to a halt, bumping over soft ground. I hoped there wasn't going to be any sort of fight about this because I was out of condition. There wasn't. The car started up again, wallowing up and down on rough grass, then stopped again. What was going on?

Another sharp smell, not petrol this time. What was it? Something familiar. Ethyl chloride. Very safe, very cautious. You could build up quite a concentration of ethyl chloride in a confined space like the trunk of a car, enough to put anyone to sleep. Me, for instance.

There seemed to be a little more space above me this time. I didn't feel quite so terrible, either. More light, too. I could make out a pattern of machining on the metal vault above me. Where was I this time? There was still a sound of engines, and suddenly the sound rose to a roar.

I was in an aircraft, a light aircraft. I shifted my arms slightly, but no dice this time, I seemed to be wrapped up in layer after layer of somebody's quilt. No, it was one of those mountain rescue stretchers they rush you down ski slopes in when you've broken a leg. I was strapped into it, laced in like a mummy, very comfortable but totally immobile. What sort of aircraft? The engine howled, the prop screamed like a banshee, we ran forward about six yards and then lifted off.

Somebody leaned over me, blocking my view of the patterned metal cabin roof. It was Pzenica.

"Okay, old boy?" he asked. What a bleeding idiotic question.

"Nice try with the lights," he said. "But too late, I think."

His head vanished from sight again. I tried to work out what size the cabin would be, about a six- or seven-seater, I thought. I would definitely take note of how long we were in the air, then I would know how far we'd flown when we touched down. Definitely a good idea. Well, about how far. Definitely.

When I woke up for the third time, the cabin door was wide open and cold air was shipping in. People got out, I couldn't tell how many. They talked in low voices, sometimes in English, sometimes not. Somebody said "no trouble at all, none," and somebody else answered "good, good, good."

They lifted me out bodily, stretcher and all. Pzenica swam into sight momentarily.

"Okay?" he said.

"No," I said.

He laughed. How come he didn't have a hangover like mine, I couldn't have laughed even if I'd felt like it. Because he burned alcohol the way other people burned food, that's why, and nobody had slipped him a Mickey Finn. We were crunching over snow.

I turned my head as much as I could. I thought the plane

was a Pilatus Porter, which meant we could be practically anywhere, because the Pilatus can land on three postage stamps, end to end. Snow meant high altitude this time of year, and so did the chill of the air. Overhead the stars blinked madly in Morse. I breathed in deeply three or four times. It was a mistake. I went to sleep again.

Twelve

THE following morning, as they say, dawned bright and clear, and a good many hours before I came to, but when I did I felt reasonably sound in wind and limb. I was in bed, for a change. I looked at my watch and found it was half past eleven.

My clothes were on a chair beside me. They were clean, dry and still warm from the iron. There was no cup of tea, but otherwise the treatment seemed to be four-star.

I got up, dressed, and went over to the window.

It was impossible to tell where I was, because this side of the house, lodge, schloss or dacha looked straight out onto the side of a mountain and I couldn't see round it. The altitude must have been six thousand feet or so. We were still in the tree line, but only just, and there was plenty of spring snow about. Over to my left it was melting briskly and filling an ice torrent with water. I could see very little more because of the bars across the window.

They would have taken about ten hours to cut even if I'd had a hacksaw. I hadn't, and they were so close together that I couldn't get my clenched fist between them, which is the professional way of doing things since then you have to cut at least two of them to get anywhere.

I turned back into the room. Waxed pine strips from floor to ceiling. Two radiators. No cupboards, no chairs except the one by the bed, no pictures, no shelves and no ornaments. As prison cells go it was comfortable, but the lock on the door confirmed that a prison cell was what it was intended to be. I sat on the bed and wished I had a magic lamp which I could rub to summon a genie, because then I could send him out for some cigarettes.

At twelve precisely there was the sound of about five bolts being withdrawn on the outside of the door. The lock turned and a fourteen-stone Neanderthal with a submachine gun appeared, dressed in a track suit. He stood aside and two men I'd seen the previous evening came into the room. I knew them as Maier the Dentist and Lizard. Both of them wore suits and guarded, neutral expressions. I couldn't decide whether I was supposed to be a reluctant guest or a full-blown political prisoner, but the general effect was to make it absolutely clear that a quick hundred-yard dash would do me no good at all.

"Good morning, I am Maier," said the Dentist, "and this is Lenk. Will you please come with us now? I hope you have been comfortable."

It sounded like an afterthought, but it's the afterthought that counts. We went along a landing and down a wide stair with military precision, Maier and Lenk on either side of me and submachine gun to the rear.

The pine strip paneling had been put on the walls of my room as an afterthought, that much was obvious. The building itself was much older and solidly made in stone. A hunting lodge modernized to make a ski lodge, perhaps? I estimated there were six rooms on this floor and there was at least one more floor above us. Through various windows I confirmed that we were high on the side of a mountain range, about fifteen hundred feet from the ridge summit, perhaps. There was still not the faintest indication of what country we were in.

We finished up, still in formation, in what was once the gun room, or perhaps the billiard room. Stone walls, tiled floor. Hanging curtains, dust and radiators everywhere. A writing table ten feet wide filled the largest bay window, and behind it sat Otto Kiess, looking small and dapper. He rose as we came in.

"Hello," he said. "And how is my old friend Major Driver? I expect he's sent you over here to drop me all sorts of useful hints, hasn't he? Do have a cigarette."

It was the first time I'd heard him speak more than two words in a row, and it was a surprise. He looked like one of those efficient, brisk Common Market businessmen who are always telling us affably that we ought to get the lead out of our boots and start coming in to work at half past seven, and his voice should have been politely accented. Instead he sounded like Oundle, Cambridge Union and somebody's p.r.o. I took one of his cigarettes, and Pzenica stepped forward from the shadowed angle by the fireplace and lit it for me.

"I was so sorry we had to bring you here in such an awkward manner. Do sit down," said Kiess. "These things tend to get a bit like a military exercise at times, but if you want to take a man from point A to point B—" he made it sound like an initiative test—"and you don't want to damage him, things can be rather difficult. You have a medical background, Dr. Yeoman, and I'm sure you'll agree I'm right."

I agreed. The quickest way of making a man unconscious is to hit him on the head. Unfortunately this process isn't as sage or as simple as one might suppose from watching television, because a certain small but important percentage of concussed men get brain hemorrhages about twenty-four hours later. Which is why one tends to keep them in hospital for observation. I didn't believe that Kiess was all that concerned about me, but it was nice of him to say so. I decided to accept it at its face value.

"Well now," he said. "You'll be wondering why we've gone to all this trouble and expense and so forth, won't you? Not to mention the discomfort to yourself." He leaned back and looked at Pzenica, who had gone back to leaning against the wall in an attitude reeking of *weltschmerz*. Kiess went on in his sales-conference voice, "It was really because I wanted to go, at some length, into this business of the T.F. Mark 2, and to put it candidly I wanted to do so on my home ground."

For an instant I genuinely couldn't think what he was talking about. I had got so used to calling it Tree Frog that I'd forgotten its official title.

I liked this less and less the more I thought about it. There is a difference, quite an important difference in my view, between the process Driver had described as 'letting a vague impression filter through to other people' and the sort of detailed discussion Kiess seemed to imply a preference for.

"I beg your pardon?" I said. It seemed about as useful as anything. I needed time.

"I expect you people have got some frightful code name for it, haven't you? Always the same, wherever you go. The Americans are the worst," said Kiess. " 'Hound Dog.' What can you do, eh? 'Hound Dog.' " He fell about laughing. Having started out on the "I beg your pardon" routine I might just as well stick with it for a while.

"I'm afraid I'm not with you yet," I said.

"Of course not," he said. "You've only just recovered from a most unpleasant journey, and I expect you've got a headache unless you're like Andre here."

He nodded in Pzenica's direction again. They seemed to have switched roles since last night. Kiess was as talkative as a jaybird and Pzenica was brooding and withdrawn. Kiess got up and rang a bell.

"What you need is some aspirin and then a good lunch," he said. "Eh?"

He was terrifyingly genial, but they marched me out in formation just the same.

It was chicken for lunch. There was a decanter of wine. No doubt if I'd been properly brought up I should have been able to deduce where I was through instant recognition of the vintage, but I couldn't. There were two white tablets by the side of the plate. They tasted like aspirin when I touched my tongue to one of them, and if I got cautious about every little thing I could very likely end up neurotic, so I swallowed them down.

I got up off the bed and tried the bars across the window

again, but they hadn't got any softer while I'd been out of the room. Or any looser either. I had better work out some plan of campaign.

I had no information to go on and they had plenty, that was the first thing. I didn't know who Kiess was, the only thing I knew about Pzenica was that someone had addressed him as "Count," and I knew less still about Maier, Lenk and the caveman with the Schmeisser. The only thing I could do, it seemed to me, was go as slowly as I could and try to pick up a few cards on the way.

The blank amazement bit, I realized, would work for about three seconds flat. After that I could either tell them all about what a wonderful machine Tree Frog was without prompting, or let them dig it out of me bit by bit by threatening to twist my arm or whatever they had in mind. After all, boosting Tree Frog was what I'd come to Europe for in the first place. It was just that I didn't know how much of a show of reluctance Driver had in mind. Maybe, I thought in a sudden flash of genius, I ought to offer to sell it to them? It seemed to be the form around here.

There was another fusillade of bolts being withdrawn. This time it was Pzenica who came in first. He had another of his large circle of friends with him.

"May I introduce a colleague?" he said. "Maxius."

Maxius was tall. Well over six feet, and the color of oiled teak. He could have stood in for Lawrence of Arabia with no trouble at all. Eyes slitted against the limitless infinite, and a small Borgia beard. He nodded.

"Maxius is expert in air engineering," said Pzenica. "It will be easier for you than talking to ridiculous amateurs, I think. Maxius has been at the Universities of Leyden and Malmö, Sweden. For the last year he was in Brazil. Okay?" He seemed to have got back some of his bounce, perhaps he only came to life in the afternoon and was hitting on all six by midnight. I didn't like the sound of Maxius. Dr. Maxius? Professor Maxius? Archbishop Maxius? I stood up.

"How do you do. I'm afraid I still don't know what all this is in aid of," I said. "But glad to meet you anyway, Dr. Maxius."

"Maxius," he said coldly. "I shall be happy to discuss your aircraft with you later. Please don't let me disturb you. Finish your lunch."

He turned and went out. I was drifting rather far from the shore, I felt, and the water was getting cold.

Midafternoon. There was no one in the gun room besides Kiess and myself. He was pleasant about the whole thing, but firm. I had stopped saying I didn't know what all this was about by half past two.

"What about the boy with the machine gun?" I asked. "Is he part of the friendly cooperation deal? Or does he come with the furniture?"

"Michael?" said Kiess. (He breathed the "H" just fractionally.) "I suppose you don't have his equivalent in Bayswater, do you? Unless that young chap Dylan is armed to the teeth, of course." He smiled, and took a second or two out for consideration. "He is part of the furniture, as you put it. I have been to a lot of trouble to get you here and I don't want you to run away. Not that there's anywhere to run to, the road isn't open yet." He was being terribly frank and open about the business. He got up from behind the gargantuan writing table and started to walk around the room. His heels clicked on the tile floor.

"It seems to me that the situation is this," he said. "My friend Driver wants you to give me some information about an aircraft. For his own reasons, naturally. Gift horses and all that, eh?"

He turned on his toes like a dancer and strode back towards me.

"Now I," he went on, "am more than happy to listen to him, which means you of course. But the position is that I must know rather more about Tree Frog than he'd like to tell me, for the moment anyway."

He grinned at me as he produced the name. I felt as though we had made about the first six moves in a chess game and I was about to make my first major and inevitable error. I was in the wrong league, that was the trouble.

"So it's merely a question of degree, I should have thought," said Kiess reasonably. "If you could be back with your friends and mine at Seeker, if you could ask them what to do, they might very probably tell you to go ahead. Don't you think?"

"Look," I said. "I've nothing to do with Seeker. You must know that. I give them advice occasionally, as a scientist. That's all."

"On this occasion, it would be the Heuser business, yes," said Kiess. I looked blank. "You don't call him Heuser? Little chap, wears terrible clothes, you know?"

"You mean Collins," I said.

"That's right, Collins."

"Yes."

I couldn't see what harm talking about Collins/Heuser would do anybody, and it might give me a lever.

"Driver had some bits of aircraft," I said. "He wanted me to try and guess where they'd come from."

"And did you?" asked Kiess.

"I told they were parts of a drone, I thought, probably a target plane," I said.

He thought this over for a bit.

"And then?" he asked.

"Then nothing," I said. "They produced some specifications, drawings and so on for a drone of ours called Tree Frog and we compared them with Collins' bits and pieces. I think Driver wanted to know if the two projects were similar or not."

"And you never actually saw Tree Frog?" said Kiess.

"No."

He tapped me, very gently, on the shoulder.

"Oh dear, oh dear, oh dear," he said. "I'm afraid you're going to have to do better than that."

He was still smiling, there was nothing menacing about him. It was as though he'd been asked to play against a weak club player for practice and I wasn't giving him much of a game.

Back in my room, I sat on the bed again. It was about nine in the evening and outside the window night was being poured over the slopes like blueberry sauce. I was beginning to get frightened and I didn't know why; it was like getting on an exposed pitch of rock even when you know you can do it. Then I realized that I was getting frightened and got angry instead.

Pzenica came at ten thirty. Mike the Schmeisser stayed outside the door and moved in behind me as I came out into the corridor.

"Look," said Kiess, "the sooner we get this over and done with, the sooner you can get back to your test tubes and whatnot and forget about the whole thing. What does it matter to you? You don't mind my asking, do you?"

I didn't mind, but I had no good answer for him. I didn't know what the hell it mattered to me.

"By the way," I said. "This is a stupid question, I know, but what are they doing back in London, keeping a light in the window for their wandering boy, or what?"

"Ah, yes," said Kiess. "I knew there was something. All that side of things has been taken care of, it's just admin. really, you know."

He rang the bell again.

"For the moment anyway," he said, "I'm afraid they aren't actually expecting you back at all. Either of you."

I turned round stupidly. Michael and Pzenica came into the gun room. They had Binnie with them.

"Miss Abrams took rather longer over the journey than you did," said Kiess. "She came the long way round."

"Well," said Binnie. "Captain Brightwell drove me to the airport."

"Yes," I said. "He did, didn't he?"

We were still in the gun room. Kiess and Pzenica had left. Michael was outside the door. I went from window to window, trying the shutters, but of course it was no use.

Yancy had asked about Collins' crashed plane. But then he might have every right to be curious about it, there was no reason to suppose that U. S. Intelligence was any slower off the mark than ourselves. I dare say they had as much information about Tree Frog as Kiess did if it came to that. Which seemed to be plenty. But Yancy had also driven her to the airport. I was getting tired and I hadn't been too bright myself, but it seemed to me that there were two large wooden arrows pointing in Yancy's direction.

"What happened then?" I asked her.

"Oh. Well there was an hour's delay before takeoff or something," she said. "So I told him not to wait, and he went away."

"He drove off, did he?" I asked. "You actually saw him drive off, I mean."

"I didn't see him get into the car and go. But why shouldn't he?"

"Never mind," I said. "What next?"

"They called my name over the speakers. When I got to the information desk a girl there, ground hostess I mean, told me there'd been an accident outside the Konigstuhl Hotel and I was to go there. Well, when I left you were all getting as high as kites. I thought—"

She broke off.

"I know what you thought. You thought I'd got blind drunk and fallen in front of a bus. Okay."

She laughed. I wished she were somewhere about a thousand miles away. She made everything just ten times as difficult by being here, but I was still pleased to see her.

"Well, something like that, I suppose," she said. "Anyway this girl found me a taxi and came with me. I didn't see which way we went or anything, but when we stopped there was an ambulance by the side of the road. Two men were carrying a stretcher into it. So I got in too. I couldn't understand what they were all saying anyway."

"And then?" I asked.

"There was nothing on the stretcher but pillows."

Easy, really. These things probably are, nearly every time.

"I suppose you don't know how long you were in the ambulance?" I asked her. But I knew the answer already. They'd just given her a bit more room for the journey than me, but the end result had been the same.

"I bloody nearly kicked one of them in the balls anyway," she said with satisfaction. She looked virtuous. Binnie was always surprising me.

Pzenica came back and took her away. I hoped she wouldn't suddenly decide to turn nasty, for his sake, because she'd probably have kicked him too, and I didn't think he looked up to her weight. But she went quietly, and Kiess came and sat down behind the writing table again.

"I told you it was purely an admin. matter," he said. "Don't worry about it. Among other things, you see, we couldn't very well have her going back to England and telling everyone where you were and who you were with when she last saw you. Could be very awkward, that sort of detail. Besides he had a convenient story for your people at the Institute."

"What story?"

"You're both dead. Presumed."

"How?"

"Oh," he said, "the usual thing. Car crash."

Sometime the next day, Pzenica came to see me.

"I hope you will not be annoyed," he said.

"What about?"

"That I say this. This is not your, what, cup of tea really, is it? I mean, you are not of the Secret Service, you know nothing of the way in which things are conducted. At least, a little, perhaps. But not much."

"What do you mean, 'a little?' "

"You didn't know?" he asked. "Otto and myself are acquainted with you, your name anyway. From 1960, you remember? Otto Kiess was in charge of some Dead Men, you know this phrase?"

I did. A Dead Man is a courier who performs minor services, usually taking things from one place to another, for a fee. He is in a way the elite among couriers, and his fee is often very high indeed, because the two essential qualities of a Dead Man are his utter reliability and his utter lack of curiosity. He rarely does anything overtly criminal, though of course he passes through Customs illegally more or less as a matter of course. Couriers who fail, even once, in reliability or curiosity, tend to lose both their livelihoods and their lives, though this is not the reason they are called Dead Men.

Otto Kiess, it appeared, had been what a friend of mine who blew safes would call a Dead Man's Ponce.

[In 1960 a man in Morocco was believed, incorrectly as it

turned out, to have synthesized a drug which produced a permanent effect on the human brain rather like a lobotomy. This effect has been achieved before, of course, by the injection of novacaine behind the eyeballs, but the effects are somewhat unpredictable, and for various reasons I was asked to go and check on the truth or otherwise of this man's claim. It took me three months, six weeks of which I spent in prison in Spain, to find out there was nothing behind the story. I didn't know Kiess was anywhere around, though I met some fairly odd characters. I came out of jail with a comprehensive dislike of intelligence work of any sort whatever. There is a saying, though, about a man and the company he keeps, and it now looked as though my name had crept into files and memories all over the place.]

I told Pzenica, carefully and in detail, exactly what my view was of the Secret Service and the way things are conducted in it. He seemed amused.

"You see? I knew you were not *simpatico*," he said. "I of course do not blame you. One man is a plumber and another an agent, it is a matter of temperament."

"I'm a scientist by temperament," I told him. "When do we get out of here so that I can go back to being a scientist and Miss Abrams to being a statistician?"

"A what?"

"A secretary," I said. I could be all day explaining what a statistician was, though I probably had all day.

"Soon," said Pzenica. "Not to worry, old boy. But tell me. If you know even a little about Secret Service work, how do you think we knew you were coming and what you were coming for?"

"All right," I said. "How?"

"Major Driver told us, of course," he said.

I suppose I knew this, and I'd been afraid of it.

In the evening I was back in the gun room. This time Kiess wasn't there, or at least I couldn't see him. The room was so huge and full of shadows that he might have been hiding anywhere.

Pzenica was at the table, and so was Maxius the Aero-engineering King, and a dark girl in glasses with a shorthand pad. She was sitting away from the light, but even if she hadn't been it would have taken me some time to recognize her. When I did, I didn't believe it.

"If we're going to get technical," I said, "would you please get rid of your secretary and replace her with a tape recorder?"

"Why?" said Maxius.

"Because I need to keep my mind on my work," I told him.

I know flexibility is vital these days and a girl ought to be able to turn her hand to anything. No doubt this is nowhere more necessary than in Intelligence, but despite the glasses and the severe, high-cut dress she still looked naked to me, and the faint scent of lemon drifted across the table and made my hands start to sweat all over again.

"I am sorry if you find her irritating," said Pzenica. He didn't see what the fuss was about.

"Skip it," I said. I didn't want them to tell me she had a Ph.D., too, and played table tennis for Rumania in her spare time.

"What is the empty weight of T.F. Mark 2?" asked Maxius.

"How should I know?" I said.

"Make a guess," said Maxius. "A reasonably informed guess."

His eyes looked out across the table at me like an owl's. He was totally uninvolved. Not only was I a lousy player but I couldn't even see the board. I took a deep breath.

"Twelve hundred pounds," I said.

Maxius nodded, and True wrote it down.

Midnight, by my watch. The room had contracted into small outposts of light in a forest of angles and shadows. The radiators hissed gently like snakes and the vast surface of the table stretched between us like the mirror surface of a dark lake. Maxius forged on, collecting, correlating, considering. By now he knew more about Tree Frog than I did, probably. To his left, Pzenica sat back into his chair, slumping his spine. He had a bottle and a glass and was drinking himself into his normal frame of mind. Beyond Maxius, True sat demurely and turned the pages of her pad.

"One last thing," said Maxius. "This aircraft is currently at —" he searched his memory for a second—"Royal Air Force, Monkham Manor. Is that correct?"

"Yes," I said. If he knew, there wasn't much point in denying it. Besides I couldn't remember if I'd told him already or not. I was tired.

"And it is, you say, in operation now?"

"Yes," I said.

"Then it must fly from Monkham Manor. Out over the North Sea, perhaps."

It was a statement rather than a question. I examined it for a bit, but I couldn't see any snags. If, as I was supposed to be maintaining, Tree Frog was actually flying (he'd tried to get me to say how many of the damned things were operational but the pitfalls here were so enormous that I'd said I didn't know, which he accepted) then we would hardly transport it somewhere else to launch it. There was a slight difficulty in that I wasn't sure I could imagine a heavy launch aircraft taking off and landing at Monkham Manor, but on balance I didn't see why not. It was an old bomber command station after all.

"That's right," I said.

"Thank you," said Maxius.

They left me in my room all next day. I had nothing to read and the view from my window was still the side of the mountain. My food was brought by Maier, the dentist (was he a dentist? He might have been) and the man who looked like a lizard and whose name was Lenk. Michael stood outside the door every time.

I was worried about Binnie. I hadn't asked for any of this, but she didn't even know it existed.

The next day it snowed. It was late in the year for it, even up here. In the afternoon the mist closed in as well and the window became a dripping wall of white. It must be Monday.

It was misty all day Tuesday. I slept a good deal of the time. When Maier came in with supper I waited until he'd put it down on the bed and was straightening up.

"Boo," I said. He jumped about six inches in the air and Michael turned in the doorway and swung the muzzle of the gun towards me and took up first pressure on the trigger. I was sorry I'd done it, but it broke up the day a little.

I woke up and knew, with certainty, that I'd missed a day, an entire twenty-four hours, asleep. Had they spiked my coffee with seconal, or was it sheer inactivity? Was I sure? Something was closing in on me, like a salmon net, a softly gloved fist.

The snow turned to rain and the mist lifted. I found that I didn't care. I wished I knew that Binnie was all right. What were they all doing? I started exercises, running on the spot, pushups, anything. I should really have been doing them all the time but I kept waiting for something to happen. Friday, was it?

Maybe the exercise was a mistake. I didn't sleep that night. I lay and looked at the ceiling and told myself that I knew what the hell they were doing all right.

In the morning I felt like a wet rag.

About five in the afternoon, if my watch was still keeping time, all the bolts shot back and I turned to the door. It was Maier and Lenk again. They marched me off, one two one two, down to the gun room. Only Kiess was there. I was surprised to find myself glad to see him.

He was in uniform, with leather belt and boots. No insignia. He was a different person, I had to look carefully at him to make sure it was Kiess after all. The big writing table had gone. How had they moved it? Where had they moved it to? It must have weighed a ton. Kiess sat behind a folding board table with a bottle of ink and some sheets of paper in front of him.

Behind his back, the shutters were closed. He was stiff, military, precise. I wasn't sure he saw me any more.

"You have been talking nonsense," he said, and rang the bell.

It was a real interrogation room this time. A prison cell. Two chairs, a small table between us. Maxius sat opposite me and didn't see me either, I was transparent. There was a barred grille in the door and another one high up in the wall behind Maxius. He was in uniform, too. The uniform was gray, there were no insignia, he was a gray stone welded to the gray stone of the cell.

"On what frequency does the T.F. Mark 2 control system operate?" he asked.

"I don't know," I said.

"You told us. The last time I was with you."

"Did I?"

I couldn't remember. I simply could not remember, all those days ago, what I'd told him, how much I'd told him, what had been the truth and what had been lies, what was fact and what I'd made up.

"You do not remember." He stated it, as a fact.

"No."

"Why do you not remember?'

"I don't believe I did tell you. I don't know what frequency it operates on."

"Very well. What materials are used in the construction of T.F. Mark 2?"

Easier ground.

"Glass fiber," I said. "Some magnesium alloy."

"This method of construction makes it a very light aircraft."

"Yes, of course it does."

"How much does it weigh?"

"Empty?" I asked.

"Yes."

"One thousand two hundred pounds."

I was getting the answers right now. It was important to get the answers right. You can't fool me.

"How much fuel does it carry?"

"One thousand six hundred pounds."

"More fuel than its own dry weight?"

"Yes," I said. I heard Sergeant Kelsey's voice. More fuel than plane, when she's fueled up and ready to go. I was getting back my grip on reality.

"The T.F. Mark 2 is a long-range reconnaissance plane," said Maxius.

"Yes," I said. "Look, what is all this? We had it out last time."

He might not have heard me. His voice was empty of any inflection.

"Since the aircraft is made largely of glass fiber and travels at a great height, it must have a very low radar reflectivity."

"Of course."

"It produces a very small echo indeed?"

"Yes."

"Which, since it is a reconnaissance craft, a spy plane, is extremely useful."

"You've got the idea," I said.

(But somewhere at the back of my mind, I could hear another voice asking these same questions, making these same statements. The voice was my own.)

"But in order to control it, you must track it on radar yourselves. Therefore you must have exceptionally powerful radar equipment in ground support. Is this true?"

"Yes, it's true," I said.

He opened a file.

"I have here an aerial photograph of Royal Air Force, Monkham Manor," he said. "This is where, you told us, the plane operates from. Here is a pencil. Will you please outline the aerials used by this powerful ground control radar system?"

He handed me the pencil and the picture. I felt as though he'd rabbit-punched me.

I looked at the map, pretending to study it, grabbing for time. I don't know where he'd got it from, but that hardly mattered now. It showed Monkham Manor for just exactly what it was, and what I knew it to be, the decayed ghost of a wartime bomber station, with cracked tarmac and pathetic, crumbling lines of Nissen huts here and there. I could see the outline of Nockolds' new wire fence and the blockhouse, but from overhead it looked just like any other compound. Vegetation of some sort was invading heaps of scrap-iron girders. One of the supply huts had a gaping hole in the roof. Farther over, the old control tower marked a pale square against the dark of the airfield itself. By it was a dish aerial.

I did the only thing I could, and ringed it with the pencil.

"Please do not be stupid," said Maxius. "That is normal approach radar of a now obsolete pattern."

"So it is," I said. I felt clumsy, stupid, like a schoolboy handing up his grubby exercise book and hoping that it will be all right this time.

"Well?" said Maxius.

"I don't know," I said. "The installation itself must be underground."

"Naturally. But the aerial arrays cannot be, can they? Or perhaps they are retractable?"

I wished I'd thought of that one first. Not that it would have done much good. He had me, and we both knew it.

"You have been talking nonsense," he said.

"That's what Kiess told me."

He stood up. He towered over me, leaned forward, his face impassive, expressionless.

"You are a British imperialist swine," he said.

It was too good to be true.

"None of us is perfect," I told him.

I slept well that night.

When I woke up, the room had changed. The bed was iron-framed, there was no radiator and the walls were stone now and streamed with damp. They must have used a barbiturate this time. The lamp overhead was armored glass nesting in wire mesh and there was no window. It was all in the best tradition.

I lay on my back and looked around. What was it today? Sunday? If I'd lost count out there, in the warmth and the light, it wouldn't take long to go right over the edge in here. Where was Binnie? Was she here at all?

I sat up and cursed Driver. Then I cursed Chapman, Beswetherick, Andy Dylan and Mrs. Maitland, and felt a bit better. But not much, and when I lay down again, the light went out.

Cold, solitary confinement and a low blood sugar are not essential to disorientation. They are not essential, but they help. I wished I could be sure of dreaming, because that way I would know when I slept and when I woke up.

The door grated open. Pzenica came in. He looked down at me.

"You do not see facts as they are," he said, "but only as you wish them to be."

When I thought about it, I could see that Kiess must have been watching and observing me in Vienna, that he had based his attack on me on what he had found out. I knew his purpose and his strategy. I knew that he was practiced in these techniques and that I was aware of them only theoretically, and that I was outclassed. For whole seconds at a time I could grasp all these things, and they made no difference at all.

"You are trained in psychology," said Kiess. "You must know that I can break you. You must know this."

He was still in uniform. We had gone back to the gun room again. It was bare; the curtain had gone, the hangings, everything. Only the hissing radiators remained, and the small, bare table and chair I sat in. The shutters were still closed. It was some time during the night, but they'd taken my watch. I knew what he said was true.

He rang the bell again and they brought Binnie into the room. Maier and Lenk held her, one on each side. There was a small, fine steel chain around her left wrist. She looked pale and the scar stood out against the rest of her skin. Kiess walked over to her and casually snapped the back of his hand against her face. His knuckles struck along the line of the scar and it started, very slightly, to bleed. She hardly moved. Michael watched from the doorway.

"You must see this as a fact," said Kiess. "We are all of us in an artificial situation, a drama, but it happens that in this artificial situation I make decisions and you do not. And who are you? You are dead people, both of you. There has been no hue and cry, no diplomatic flurry, no questions have been asked."

He came over to my chair.

"Be reasonable," he said. "You are a rational man, a scientist. If I wish to have you killed, I can do so. If I wish to give the girl to Michael I can do that too." He flicked his fingers under his chin. "She is by no means pretty," he said, "but then Michael is no oil painting."

He was smiling, and I could sense a certain complicity in his smile; it was as though he were inviting me to take part in some game that he could understand and I could not. I studied him as carefully as I could and I looked at his picture of things, and suddenly I could see that all he was was a little man who liked beating up girls and that was all there was to it. There was nothing much I could do, but it was a help. I slid down in the chair and sideways scissored my legs in front of his and behind, and he toppled forward and dragged the chair over onto both of us. Michael came across the room at a run, holding the gun by the muzzle like a golf club, and I could do nothing but watch as he swung it down towards my head.

I thought he must have split the side of my skull open, but he hadn't. I felt it with the tips of my fingers and then left it alone. The overhead light was out and the cell felt like a coffin.

Michael hauled the door open and put a tray on the floor. He smiled amiably at me and I asked him what time it was. He stopped smiling and heaved the door shut again.

Thirteen

THERE was no light on in the interrogation cell, either, and they'd boarded over the window grilles. I sat in the dark with Maxius, each on our own side of the table. I was free to get up and go any time, the door of the cell was open, but I didn't.

"Why did you tell us all that nonsense?" asked Maxius, and hit me. I only felt it when he hit me on the side of my face which was bruised from the gun, and even then I didn't feel it much.

"Why?" asked Maxius.

"I don't know," I said.

"There must be a reason," he said.

"There is, but I forget what," I said. I was almost asleep.

"You are an English imperialist swine," he said.

"I'm not interested in politics," I told him, and he swung at me again in the soft, liquid darkness and I hardly objected to it at all. I dropped my head on the table and went to sleep.

There was a face opposite me, on its side, I could just see the outline of the jaw. The face was youngish and had beard bristles like a hedgehog, and white eyes.

"Forgive me, for I have sinned," it said. "Forgive me."

I shut my eyes again. A hand gripped my shoulder and rolled me to and fro and my face dropped against the metal bed frame.

"Forgive me," said the face. "I have sinned."

"We are all sinners," I said. "Now belt up."

"It's Phillips, sir," said the face. I still didn't believe it was there. "You remember me, sir, don't you? Phillips."

"Okay Phillips," I said. "Just relax and let me get some sleep, will you?"

He shook me again. For Pete's sake, I thought. What now?

"Sir. Take me home with you when you go, sir, will you? You remember me, don't you? Phillips?"

I shook my head, opened my eyes wide, closed them, opened them again. There was a tiny glow from the overhead light, hardly enough to see by.

"Listen, Phillips," I said. "I'll take you home okay, but if you don't give it a rest right now I swear to you that I am going to punch you right on the nose."

It made no difference at all. The face was the right way up now as I sat on the side of my bed in the cell.

"I'd deserve that," said Phillips. "I've sinned and I know I'd deserve it, only take me back with you when you go."

The man with the face called Phillips squatted in the far corner of the cell and went on asking me to take him home until, hours later, Michael opened the door and told him to come out, and he set up a thin, ferrety screaming and then went out without looking at me and the door shut again. There is a point which can be reached when it is of no importance, none at all, to inquire whether one is mad or not, whether one is having hallucinations or not. I closed my eyes again.

I told Maxius all about Tree Frog, that it was a development aircraft, that it could fly all right but nobody had yet developed a means of long-range command control that would work, that I didn't know when they would or if they could. I told him that Driver had sent me over to spread the rumor that it could be controlled and was in operational use.

"Why should he do that?" asked Maxius.

I told him I didn't know, that I was tired and they could fight it out between them. He told me I was a British imperialrialist swine.

"I do not believe you," he said. "You are asking me to believe that the British Government has developed, at a cost of millions of pounds, a pilotless aircraft which they have no means of controlling. This is ridiculous."

I told him he could work it out whichever way he chose, I didn't care. I'd told him the facts and that was that. He told me that he didn't believe me and that I was a British imperialist swine and a liar.

I woke up again. I felt much better, dangerously better, as though I were on the other side of a mirror. I was in my old room again, the one with the barred windows and the pine-strip walls, and the bed was comfortable.

My mind was clear. I sat up, remembering the dream about the face called Phillips. I fingered my own chin thoughtfully.

I had told lies and been disbelieved. I'd told the truth and been disbelieved, and I didn't like to think about where I was going from here. My mind seemed to be poised, as though on an edge. Outside it was just getting dark. I stood up. I was weak.

Michael came in by himself this time. He was smiling again and I found out, this time, that he could talk too.

"Eat," he said. He was carrying a tin tray and the gun was slung across his shoulder. I thanked him.

"Not thank me." He went right on smiling, cheerfully and proudly. "You are British imperialistiki swine," he said, and because I could now see, clearly and truly, that I was, I knew I had to escape and it had to be now.

He stooped and put the tray down on the bed. I did the only thing I could think of, and took the four steps between us at a run, slamming my head and shoulder into his hips. He was just off balance and his head thudded into the wall by the bed, caving in two of the pine planks. He grunted and slumped over the tray. Soup dripped to the floor and I hoped he wasn't dead because I needed him. I grabbed the broken soup bowl and with one of the sharp edges hacked through the strap of the gun because it was easier to do that than try to roll him over and work it off him. He started to groan and thrash about and I jammed the muzzle of the gun between his teeth and the cold metallic taste woke him.

Fourteen

I could understand why he'd got careless. I hadn't done much but even so I felt as though I'd been in a pitched battle.

I held the gun firm while he came round and almost bit the last inch off the barrel with shock. I didn't blame him, but people had been messing me around too much lately for me to care about the way he felt. His teeth clicked against the foresight as I stepped back. His eyes flickered from side to side, but he read the code all right.

"You understand me," I said.

He nodded.

"Where is the girl?"

He looked up and then pointed towards the ceiling. I didn't move my eyes to follow his movement, because I knew I only needed to make one small mistake now and that would be it. His head was like a cannonball and I expect the wall took more harm than his skull when he butted it, so I wasn't taking chances.

I gestured slightly with the gun and he stood up, wincing. I was glad to see we were on the same frequency. He knew I was in plenty of trouble but he could see that all the medals they'd pin on him wouldn't stop up the holes in his chest if he didn't cooperate. He looked at the gun and I hoped he hadn't left the safety catch on.

We went out into the corridor and then turned upstairs instead of down. The Schmeisser MP 38 is a rich cousin of the Sten but the magazine clips on underneath, which makes the balance different. I followed him just far enough away so that he couldn't kick back at me, but he'd shrunk without his gun and now he only looked like a fat, stupid man in a combat jacket.

At the top of the stairs he turned right. Only one of the doors on the top landing was bolted on the outside so I knew this must be the one. I signed for him to pull the bolts back. I still couldn't feel any of this was real, and maybe he saw this in my eyes, because he did as he was told. I lifted the gun slightly and we went in.

The room they'd put her in looked no more comfortable or uncomfortable than mine had been. She was sitting on the bed with a band-aid over the cut on her temple. When she saw me behind Michael she stood up; there was a very faint metallic rattle from the fine chain on her wrist which held her to the bed.

Of course I forgot and dropped my guard. I looked at her to see if she was all right, and Michael suddenly stopped being fat and stupid and a fraction of a second later he had both hands on the Schmeisser across his body. I seemed to have all the time in the world. I let go of the barrel, which left his hands full and mine empty, and went for his eyes with my thumbs. None of this was very edifying, but he was bigger than me and I didn't have time to worry about the ethics of gouging.

He grunted and dropped the gun, as he had to. Every animal protects its eyes. As he rocked backward, clutching at his face, I pushed him and he tripped over the chair and fell against the bed. His head struck the frame with a thump of finality. Twice in five minutes is enough for anyone.

I looked at the chain on Binnie's wrist. There didn't seem to be much point in it, the links were so small, but when I tried to do something about it I found they were made of tempered steel. In the end we had to twist part of it around the bed frame and use the barrel of the Schmeisser as a lever, but it broke.

"What's happening?" she asked.

I nearly laughed, but I didn't really feel like it.

"It's all part of the war," I said.

"What war?"

"A private one," I told her, "and you and I are getting out of it."

"You look worn out," she said.

"I am worn out. But I'm in a hurry. Help me get his jacket off."

"What for?" she asked.

"If you ask me what for just once again," I said, "I'll leave you here to find out the answers."

We got his combat jacket off quite easily, but his boots and trousers were more difficult. Binnie didn't look as though she was used to this sort of thing. His shirt tore, but I put it on just the same, over my own.

"The jacket and trousers are for you," I told her. "The boots are mine."

She started to say something, but looked at me and thought better of it.

"Do I have to take my skirt off?"

I considered the matter as judicially as I could.

"Leave it on," I said. "There's plenty of room in those trousers for it and you." She was a big girl, but even so she looked lost in Michael's top layer of clothes. I hoped they'd keep her warm. The shirt I had smelled strongly of goat. His boots were the right size for me, which was a bonus.

I shoved her out onto the landing and bolted the door on the outside. I hadn't the faintest idea what I was going to do next, but I hoped she couldn't tell. I tried the next door along the passage, which turned out to be a broom cupboard. The next one was a storeroom of some sort.

"In here," I said.

It must have been the caretaker's top-floor refuge from the harsh world of dust and doorknobs. There was a light wooden chair and table, and in one of the cupboards I found a tin of polish with an Italian label, a box of rags, a paper bag which seemed to be full of sugar, half a pint of sour milk and some cheese straws.

I tipped about two ounces of sugar into the palm of my hand and crammed most of it into my mouth. I washed it down with about half the milk and told her to do the same. She made a face at the milk but got it down. I shoved the cheese straws inside my shirt and then tried the window. It was stuck.

There was a voice from downstairs, shouting.

I took the chair and the table and jammed them against the door and shot the inside bolt. It would stop anybody real determined to get in for about ten seconds. There was a rope stretched across the room with a pair of socks draped over it to dry, and I undid it, wrapped it around my fists and slammed at the window frame. The whole thing fell outwards with a crash, and I could hear the shouting voices much better. I coiled the rope around my waist and looked out.

I knew we were on the same side of the house as I'd been in my room downstairs. This meant that we were in the more or less permanent shade of the slope, and with any luck there'd still be lots of snow. We were on the second floor, but that doesn't mean much if you're against the side of a mountain. Ten feet below the window, the ground floor snow-eaves projected out. They sloped too much to stand on, of course, but they were covered with snow, how much I couldn't tell.

It was still the quickest way down, and the furore downstairs told me it might be the safest, too.

"Out," I said to Binnie. She didn't argue, and right then and there I made up my mind about her.

When she was about halfway through the window, feet first, I pushed her hard without giving her time to think. She screamed and vanished from sight. I heard feet thundering along the landing outside. Somebody was shouting, "Mikhail, Mikhail." It sounded like Maier.

The lock of the door rattled and there was a crash of some hardy soul throwing a shoulder against it. I slipped the catch of the Schmeisser to single-shot and fired at the door.

There was an even louder shout from the other side. I jumped for the window and hauled myself through. I couldn't see Binnie, it was too dark now, but I could see where she'd bounced off the snow-eaves all right. I threw the Schmeisser out into the darkness and jumped. My feet struck the eaves and I rolled backward and out from the side of the house in a parachutist's reflex. As I arced out I hoped there was lots of nice soft snow to land in.

There was. I fought my way out of a deep bank of the stuff, spitting, and called softly, "Binnie?" I don't know why I bothered to drop my voice, we'd already made enough noise to start an avalanche. Even slogging through Flittermouse Three would be an easier way of making a living.

I heard her call from about ten yards away to my left. I asked her if she was hurt and got a two-word reply not often heard from girls even these days. I hunted around and thought I'd found the Schmeisser until I cut my hand and realized it was the remains of the window I'd pushed out. The gun was a few feet farther on, three-quarters buried in snow, and as I gripped it there was a whipcrack from overhead. Somebody had got into the storeroom. I don't know where the bullet went, but it was nowhere near me.

I remembered the sergeant instructor at Bisley addressing me and a bookish squadron leader (Secretarial) as we stood on the range with our Sten guns and our yearly compulsory supply of ammunition, small arms, Ground Officer Training. "Don't forget you're the Queen's paid killers, gentlemen," he'd said. It had seemed unlikely at the time. Now, I pushed the catch back to repeat, sighted vaguely in the direction of the third-floor window and squeezed the trigger. The Schmeisser bucked and threw high and to the right, just like the Sten always did. In my opinion the Sten is strictly for laughs if you're thinking in terms of actually hitting anything with it, but it's quite good at clobbering things in a bomb-happy Maquis sort of way, and I hoped I'd discourage whoever it was up there from sticking their heads out of the window for a while.

I kicked my way across to where Binnie was waiting. I told her to run for the trees, two hundred yards away on the other side of the mountain stream, and she nodded and set off. Few girls are built for running but she did her best.

I came in to the wall of the house and slid along it after her. I'd nearly reached the corner when Lenk pushed up a ground-floor window, stuck his head out and loosed off some sort of pistol at me. I gave the trigger of the Schmeisser a minimum pull and got off about three rounds in his direction and his head disappeared, and someone upstairs again saw the muzzle flashes and started to rake the ground to one side of me with automatic fire. I was glad I'd come in under the eaves even if it meant close work with Lenk.

Enough is enough, though. I turned and ran, which is what I was much more suited for. I splashed across the stream, slipped on a boulder and nearly wrenched my ankle, and then I was up and running for the trees across the airstrip.

I didn't know if I'd hit Lenk. I hoped that nobody with a good rifle had me lined up in a set of night sights because a rifle is for real. Then I was in among the trees and Binnie said, "Me friend, no shoot," and I leaned against the trunk of a pine and sucked in great whistling gasps of breath. The freezing night air sliced into my lungs like a razor. I knew we couldn't stop. Not because of the guns pointing in our direction but because of the cold.

I heard another clatter of shots from the house, but they might just as well have been shooting at air for all the good it would do them now. I felt around my chest. At least three of the cheese straws had survived the trip and I gave them to Binnie and brushed crumbs from all over me.

"Excuse fingers," I said.

Fifteen

FIVE minutes later, I still hadn't made up my mind. Indecision is the cause of a good deal of grief. So is being decisive and coming up with the wrong answer.

"What happens now?" asked Binnie.

"Well," I said. "If we were on television it would be easy. We'd make a swift, silent dash for that plane there, I should haul you aboard, gun the engines, there'd be a quick sting of mood music and we'd soar into the night sky. As we aren't, it wouldn't work out that way. We'd get there all right, it would take me two minutes to work out which was the starter and another three to discover how you're supposed to get the engine firing from cold. By the time we'd found out that the damn thing hasn't been refueled, there would be a big ring of guns all pointed at our heads."

"I'm getting frozen," she said.

It was all very well. I looked around. Behind us was the ridge. How far to the top? Fifteen hundred feet?

I thought I heard a shouted conversation from over by the lodge, but nobody was setting up a hue and cry after us. One reason was that it was dark, and another that it was cold.

Not as cold as all that, but there was a thin layer of cloud over the sky and I knew we'd have to get away by morning or we'd be sitting ducks when daylight came.

"How long ago did you last eat?" I asked her. "Before those cheese straws?"

"Just before you came into the room."

That was something. I'd missed my meal. Michael had fallen all over it, but the sugar I'd shoveled into myself in the caretaker's room would help. Not much, but it would help.

I unslung the Schmeisser and took off Michael's shirt.

"Your feet are wet," I said.

"What about you?" she asked.

I told her that a wet overshirt wouldn't worry me, but that wet feet would do her no good at all. She was wearing reasonable shoes, that was something. I don't say she could go for a twenty-mile hike in them but at least they were designed to travel over short distances without falling to pieces or crippling her.

I took them off one at a time. She was wearing stockings under Michael's denim trousers, and there wasn't much I could do about that. I rubbed her feet briskly with the shirt, took off Michael's boots and gave her my socks. I wasn't mad about the idea of clambering about in boots and no socks, but I've climbed in bare feet before now. I put the damp shirt back on again. The facts were still that I wasn't dressed for mountaineering and Binnie wasn't shod for it, and it was madness at the best of times to go scrambling about at this sort of altitude in the dark.

I wanted, badly, to put distance between us and the lodge.

I knew, because I could still feel it, how nearly Kiess and Maxius had come to pushing me over the edge into total compliance. I could remember what I'd told Maxius in the velvet darkness and I still had no sense of failure, because it had been someone else who'd told him. Now I wanted distance between us, and if possible at least one major obstacle. If we stayed at this level until tomorrow they'd have a plane and at least five men looking for us.

I wished I knew what country we were in. On balance, but only just on balance, I thought we'd still be this side of the East-West watershed, because of the difficulties involved in getting both of us across it. But Vienna is very close to the edge of things and I wasn't sure.

"Come on," I said to Binnie.

We worked our way through the trees, gaining a little height. There was still no sign of pursuit, and I thought of Kiess and his precise and tactical little mind and I could see why not. Only idiots mount posses and charge around in the dark after the first enthusiasm has worn off.

After about ten minutes or so we reached the far edge of the wood. I looked up and surveyed the ridge summit. My mind told me not to go upward into the cold and the open, but my instinct pulled that way just the same.

There were a dozen things I ought to have done. Sabotaged the plane. Looked in it to see if there were any binoculars, more clothes, at least got a squint at the compass. I'd done none of these things. All I'd done was run like hell.

There was a notch in the summit itself and a gully leading vaguely up in that direction, but you never can tell if they connect and a wise man doesn't bet on it.

I could look after myself in most mountain conditions. The decisions I made now would be for both of us, Binnie as well as myself, and the penalties for deciding wrong were severe. I knew what the risks were and just why you shouldn't climb at night, in snow, in unfamiliar terrain and totally ill-equipped. What I wanted was a compass, a powerful torch, sixty feet of one-and-a-quarter-inch Viking, a water flask, iron rations, a map, gloves, helmet and crampons. What I had was Binnie and twelve feet of clothesline. Plus a Schmeisser submachine gun which was getting heavier by the minute and was probably about as much use to me as a spud-gun.

"We're going up, love," I said. "Up there."

I pointed, and she tried to see where I meant, though it made no odds to her.

"All right," she said.

It had a lot in common with Russian roulette. If the weather had changed, if it had frozen harder or snowed or if the wind had risen, we would have died. It was as simple as that. If the climb had reached any level of difficulty higher than Moderate, which is the Climbers' Club's polite way of labeling an afternoon stroll, we'd have died too, just as we'd have done if there'd been a fall of rock or snow. But none of these things happened.

We climbed inside the gully for most of the way, roping out once to avoid an overhang but that was all. The rope wouldn't have held so much as a slip from either of us, but we had to keep moving or freeze and it was easier to stop

Binnie thinking about what she was doing if there was a rope between us.

It took us a bit more than two hours to reach the ridge, the notch wasn't choked with snow and there weren't any cornices. As we turned the ridge the moon came out. Binnie came and sat with her cold hands under my clasped arms, and I looked down the reverse slope of the ridge, along a broad sweep of scree and snow, and saw the refuge hut far out to the left of us, on a shoulder. She was tired out and I was still three-quarters starved, but I knew we'd make it.

Sixteen

THE refuge hut seemed empty, though the door wasn't locked. Which meant that it was a genuine high-altitude refuge, whatever country we were in.

Lower down, the mountain huts are visited more frequently and often have caretakers, but up here people were evidently trusted not to break the place up for firewood or leave picture magazines and lollipop sticks around. And to take what food and fuel they needed and pay for it, now or later. All these things add up to a way of life found only above seven thousand feet these days, and the world is seething higher and higher up the slopes every year, at least along the lines stitched by the cable cars and chair lifts.

I pushed open the door. It was cold but roomy, and two kerosene lamps hung just inside. There was no hut-keeper. Perhaps it was just as well. The Schmeisser is not a well-recognized item of climbing gear, though the only hut-keeper I know well, Franz Hochmeister, claims to have been visited by the Archangel Gabriel, and wouldn't have turned a hair.

I could feel sanity returning slowly. There was a pressure cooker and two large kerosene stoves, and I filled a kettle with snow, packed hard, and set it to melt and then boil. There was black bread and tinned butter, sausage, tea, and the universal Nestle's condensed milk. I wandered through to the back room, damp and musty with stored rugs and climbing skins. There was a map on the wall. I held the lamp up to it. We were in the Oeztal Alps, southwest of Innsbruck, and I started to shake with relief and then went back to the other room and told Binnie.

I still didn't know what time it was, but this time I didn't really care. I was human again. I cleaned and polished the mechanism of the Schmeisser without any longer feeling that the bloody thing was part of me. Binnie sat at the edge of the globe of light and warmth which held us in, drinking tea from a tin mug which she held cupped between her palms, and watched me unwind.

"I'll tell you something," I said.

"What?"

"If you woke up one fine morning," I said, "and felt, all of a sudden, that you had to be a hero or burst, you'd never find a way to make it, not by yourself. It's only other people who think up ways to make you a hero, and each way they come up with is a damn sight more idiotic than the last. It's the same with wars," I told her, "some raving twit waves his hand and sends everybody over the top, out of their nice safe little foxholes, and two minutes thought would have saved them all the trouble. I've never been sold on democracy but there's getting to be something very attractive in the idea of one man, one vote."

She didn't say anything. The room smelled of smoke and

kerosene and the hot metal of the stoves. I knew we weren't out of the woods yet, but it could wait until morning.

"Nobody's told me what we're doing here yet," she said finally. "Is that it? Is that what you're doing, being a hero?"

"You bet your sweet life," I said. "Except that when it came to finals I didn't quite make it. But you're doing all right, love, and it's better to be a heroine in a cause you know nothing about, because that way you can be one without being a half-wit as well."

There were twelve rounds left in the Schmeisser and I clipped the magazine back in place. The band-aid had come off her temple some time during the long scramble over the ridge, but in the soft yellow light from the kerosene lamps the scar was nearly invisible. She looked calm and amiable, as she might have looked in her tiny office at the Institute.

"There's a man in London who can tell you what it's all about," I said.

"Why not you?" she asked.

"Because I don't know all the answers, or even most of them. And the ones I do know don't make it worth the trouble." I thought of what it did add up to when I'd tried to work it out. Twenty million pounds of somebody's money in R. and D. appropriations.

Even I still didn't think it was worth it, and in a way I was a volunteer. Well, in a way. Binnie, on the other hand, had been given no choice at all. She stood up.

"What I need is a bath," she announced. She took one of the lamps and went out of the room.

"You could always try rolling in the snow," I called after her. "It always works wonders in Finland."

I went over and pulled back one of the wooden shutters, looking out across the snow. It must be somewhere between one in the morning and four, I thought. There was nothing out there to remind me where we'd come from. It was a night like many other nights I have spent in mountain huts, except that this time I had a submachine gun on the floor beside me.

Below the window was the first flag-marker pointing the long climb down to the valley floor. In places the snow had been thrown up into heaps and packed hard, but there were no fresh footprints except our own. Nobody had been here since the snowfall a few days ago.

The ground fell away steeply on three sides of the rock shoulder. I couldn't see any flat area large enough to put the Pilatus down on, which was a help. I ought to have been feeling tired to the bone, but I wasn't. Now that I'd eaten, I was even tempted for an instant to start down the mountain, to set still more time and more distance between ourselves and any pursuit. But the temptation to run until you drop is one that besets all fugitives, and I knew it. *Morgen ist auch ein tag.* Tomorrow is another day, and sufficient unto the day is the evil thereof.

I heard a movement behind me, and turned. Binnie came back into the room, clutching a pile of blankets, and dropped them on the gently sloping wooden sleeping bench which ran round three walls of the room in a continuous curve. It's not a very comfortable arrangement, but it serves for one man or thirty.

She had taken off Michael's combat jacket and overtrousers when we arrived, and now she had left her blouse and skirt in the other room too.

"I thought of sleeping through there, but it's cold," she said. She sounded practical. Overpractical, perhaps, but it was too dark for me to read her expression. She put the kerosene lamp down on the floor and straightened, turning slightly away from me, and her freckled, battered cat-face vanished in the darkness so that all I could see was her one hundred and fifty pounds of strong and beautifully balanced swimmer's body. I'd forgotten what a big girl she is, my mind told me inconsequentially. It's a damned good thing she didn't slip or the rope would never have held and that's for sure.

She sat down on the blanket on the sleeping bench and looked straight at me.

"I haven't got a thing to wear," she said.

"Never mind."

"I don't."

Seventeen

SOME time after first light the Pilatus flew overhead. I barely heard it, but I slid my arm out from under her shoulder and rolled over, checking that the Schmeisser was close at hand. The sound of the turboprop engine faded and then died suddenly as the plane passed over a ridge somewhere. I sat with my back to the wall for about an hour, looking at Binnie. I didn't want to wake her.

We were halfway down to the valley by the time the sun came up. Five minutes later the steep mountain path joined a forestry *Ziehweg* and the going became easier. I kept thinking that we weren't safe yet, that Pzenica or Kiess would step out from behind one of the trees beside the trail and the nightmare would begin all over again, but nothing happened.

The trail became a lane and then a road, and I had almost fallen asleep again when a Haflinger truck buzzed to a halt beside us. A head wearing a brown woolen cap shot out of the cab window and the driver stared at us. He went on staring and took in the Schmeisser. Perhaps he didn't believe it. We must still have looked like the English abroad though, because he said "Can I give you two a ride anywhere?"

He was a New Zealander, and he was going back to start a mountaineering school in South Island when he'd finished climbing every Alp in sight. Binnie sat next to him in the cab of the Haflinger and talked about her cousin in Auckland, and once he leaned across her and spoke to me.

"Do you carry that thing everywhere?" he asked.

I told him I didn't and that I didn't need it any more, and that if he'd stop the truck I'd get rid of it. I dropped it in a ditch full of green scummy water and watched the bubbles rise from the end of the barrel as it tilted and sank into the mud, and then he drove us on into Innsbruck. Nobody was pleased to see us because we had no passports, no means of identification and no money, but they let me make a phone call to London.

A little after twelve Andy Dylan arrived. I don't know what he told the authorities and by then we were past caring.

We were all back in Bayswater before dinner.

Eighteen

"Of course if you really want to go back, there's nothing much we can do to stop you," said Andy.

"I'm glad to hear it," I told him. "I was beginning to think your powers were unlimited."

"Just ill-defined," he said. "It often comes to the same thing in the end."

He grinned at me, unperturbed. Twenty-four hours ago I was jumping out of a second-floor window in Austria, or perhaps Italy, I'd need a map to pinpoint it exactly. But that was twenty-four hours ago. Here and now, at 10 P.M. in the cellar at Olsen's, the younger set were just beginning to surface before moving on to whatever orgies of rape and drug-taking we must all presume them to spend their nights wound up in. They looked a cheerfully harmless bunch to me, though right now they made me feel about a hundred years old. I'd had a hard day.

I looked down at my evening paper. THIRTY POISONED BY SCOTCH EGGS.

There was no real reason why I shouldn't have told Andy to jump in the lake as soon as he'd got us through Customs at

Heathrow, but I hadn't. For one thing half my notes for Flittermouse Three were in my temporary office at Seeker. I still felt light-headed. It was difficult to decide which was reality, this or the whispered midnight sessions with Kiess and Maxius.

"Where's your National Insurance card?" I asked.

"What?"

"Your insurance card. You've heard of them, haven't you, or don't they fit into the scheme of things over the road? I'm just curious to know who holds, examines and stamps Secret Service agents' insurance cards, that's all."

"Miss Maitland's got it. Don't be bloody silly," said Andy. He looked at me as though he were going to have to write some sort of report on my mental condition and didn't know what to put on it. I felt rather disappointed. The place was starting to fill up steadily. Girls in Marks and Spencers shirts and boys in denim waistcoats were pouring relentlessly down the stairway as though from a funnel.

"Who pays you?" I asked.

"Why?"

"Curiosity."

"The Sovereign in person," he said. "It's been on the Statute Book since George the Third and nobody's bothered to get it changed. Civil List."

"I see. Thank you."

"You don't mind if I ask what all this is in aid of?" said Andy.

"I just wanted to know if there was anyone I could complain to if I didn't like my working conditions," I told him. "But I can see that it isn't going to do me much good."

"You could try the P.M.," he said.

He looked a bit hot and bothered, and his collar was starting to wilt. The cellar was now at body temperature, so it might have been that. I knew that he'd been sent along to ensure that I did what Driver wanted me to do, and I felt sorry for him and irritated with him in alternate five-minute bursts.

"It was tough, was it?" he asked.

"It was all valuable new experience," I told him. "Let's leave it at that, shall we?"

"Worse than that Spanish jail?"

"Don't make me laugh," I said. "They knew they were going to have to let me out of that jail as soon as anybody came round and told them I was a simple innocent English lad. They gave me fifty cigarettes a day and copies of Lorca in the original Spanish to keep my mind off the heat."

"Oh," he said. "It wasn't too bad, then." He reminded me of someone who's come hospital visiting and can't think of anything to say.

Two girls crammed themselves in behind my chair. One was fat and the other thin. They were both heavily made up around the eyes and looked about thirteen.

"The worst thing about it was the fact that everybody seems to think I'm dying to do it all over again," I said. "You, Driver, Chapman and that creep from M.I.6 or whatever they call it these days—"

"Sloane?" He sounded as though it was the Chief Scout.

"Yes, Sloane. You're all under the impression that doing a spot of part-time intelligence work is just my idea of a holiday. You're wrong. It's not. What I want from the Austrian

Alps is a fortnight's rock and ice work every now and again, not a ten-day dry-cleaning session for my tired scientific brain."

The fat girl giggled and turned round, jamming her elbow into my ribs because there was no other place for it to go. I don't think she meant to, it was just that she was interested in other peoples' lives. Andy glared at her, and then at me. I knew he was dying to tell me to keep my voice down, but he bounced right back after a second or two.

"Patriotism dictates," he said.

"Don't give me that," I said. "I'm a Welsh nationalist, or didn't you know? I've got a plan to put an unknown bacteria in the Birmingham Corporation reservoir and turn everybody bright green."

"I'll get you another cup of coffee," he said.

He got up and fought his way to the counter. Both the fat girl and the thin girl were looking at me with interest.

"We're rehearsing," I told them. "Television script. It's a new series."

"Bit noisy down here, though," said the fat girl. "I mean you can't hear yourself speak, can you? Except you, you're shouting your head off."

"It's atmosphere stuff," I said. "He's brilliant but he's a nut. Can't direct a show without getting the feel of the whole thing first."

"Go on. He's a television director, then, is he?" said the thin girl.

"He's too young," said the fat one.

"New wave," I said.

When he came back with the coffee I stood up and fought my way out past both the girls.

"Where are you going?" Andy asked. He looked twitchy as hell. I suppose if I vanished he'd get his pips torn off or something.

"Don't worry," I said. "I'm going to report for duty all right."

As I went upstairs I heard the thin girl say "Are you a director, then?" I left them to sort it out between them and walked the half mile or so back to Seeker.

I climbed the stairs to Beswetherick's office in a sour frame of mind. Beswetherick wasn't there himself. Sloane and Driver were, together with Christopher Greve-Gillett. At least he wasn't wearing his chalk-stripe suit.

"Hello, Giles," he said. "Nice to see you here."

He held out his hand. He'd been assistant to the Chief Scientist during the Farnborough stretch of my life and we'd run across each other, in a spirit of mutual tolerance, many times. He was believed to go to bed regularly at half past nine and I wondered how they'd got him here this late at night. I don't know if the belief was true, but he was undoubtedly on the ball by six thirty every morning, which gave him an edge over nearly everybody else in morning conferences, and the belief may have arisen from natural envy.

"What are you doing here?" I asked.

"Oh, well," he said, waving a hand like a palm frond gently to and fro in the air, "you know."

Driver and Sloane sat on either side of him. It looked the

basis of a public inquiry, or perhaps a court-martial. I felt my temper rising.

"No, I don't," I said. "Have you come to see fair play, or what?"

"Something like that," he said.

I turned to Driver.

"There's only one thing I want to know from you," I said. "Who arranged for Miss Abrams to come to Vienna as my secretary?"

"Yes. We were rather sorry about that," said Driver. "Though as a matter of fact it was your director's idea. Dr. Michaelson. We couldn't very well oppose it without tipping our hand."

"Not that you wanted to."

"My dear chap."

"Listen," I said. "Not that there's going to be a next time, but if anything like that ever happens again there's going to be such a scream that everyone from the Security Commission to the Royal Mint will be down on your heads like a ton of bricks."

"My dear chap," said Driver again, "what could we do about it?"

"Stopped her coming."

"Mm. You must see that it was hardly in our interests to have her in Vienna with you. The last thing we wanted was for undue pressure to be brought to bear on you."

"For all I know," I said, "you might have wanted her back here afterwards to check whether I'd done my job properly."

"Really," said Greve-Gillett. "You surely don't think—"

"Oh yes, I do," I said. "All this is way out of my class, but one thing is obvious even to my tiny, simple mind. Intelligence work sometimes gets nasty and messy. If the Russians were the only people who were nasty about it, then either we'd be way behind or else we're much cleverer than they are to make up for it. With respect to all present, I doubt if we're much cleverer. Therefore we're just as nasty."

"Nevertheless," said Greve-Gillett. He had a habit of producing just this word and nothing else. Like Humpty Dumpty, it meant what he chose it to mean, and in this case it meant there's a nice knockdown argument for you. Driver gave me a look as though I were a performing seal and if I went on doing as well he'd throw me a nice lump of fish. Sloane didn't move a muscle.

"What did you eventually tell them?" asked Driver.

"The lot," I said. "Everything I knew about Tree Frog and a few bright guesses thrown in as well to keep them happy."

Driver didn't seem disturbed, but Greve-Gillett looked as though he'd just found a tadpole in his soup.

"Not really?" he said. He annoyed me. I knew it was probably just defensiveness on my part, but I couldn't help it. I looked across the table at him.

"They had a tame aeronautical engineer there, a man called Maxius," I said.

"Maxius." Sloane came briefly to life, opposite Driver. "Maxius," he said again. It wasn't even a comment. He seemed to be flicking through a million punched cards in his mind.

"If your lot couldn't even fool me with your piece about Tree Frog being fully operational, how long do you think I was able to fool him?" I went on. "He tore the whole phony story to bits in nothing flat. He even had aerial photographs of Monkham Manor," I said to Driver, "in case you're interested."

"Inevitable," he said wearily. "Inevitable. I understand your position, old boy."

"Okay then," I said. "Let's not sit around as though I'd committed high treason. It was your goof, not mine. After he'd torn it to ribbons I had to tell them something."

"Quite," said Driver. "In any case, there is no conceivable reason why you should have been able to withstand the methods which I gather Kiess used."

"You don't get the message yet, do you?" I said. "Kiess didn't have to brainwash me, he was just wasting time. All he had to do was say he'd shoot me at dawn the following day if I didn't cooperate. Don't confuse me with the brave bunch of lads you usually work with. I'm strictly an amateur."

"You did well enough in the Morocco business," said Greve-Gillett.

"Not you as well," I said. "Perhaps after my performance so far in *this* business you'll cross me off the list again, will you?"

There was a short silence. After a bit Greve-Gillett snapped briskly into action, stuffing papers into his briefcase. One of the files, I saw, was labeled TREE FROG TRIALS PROCEDURE and underneath that, in smaller lettering, AL Q.

"I think that's all, then, isn't it?" he said judicially. "Driver?"

"Fair enough," said Driver. They were all being terribly

decent about the whole thing. "Though we did still want Dr. Yeoman's assistance in the next phase."

"Yes indeed," said Greve-Gillett.

"What sort of assistance?" I asked.

"Well," said Driver, "for a start, we wanted you to stay here, lie low for a bit. That is, if you're still willing to carry things a stage further."

"What about Miss Abrams?"

"Oh, yes, Miss Abrams," said Driver. "She has agreed to keep out of the way for a week or so."

"Why should she do that?" I asked.

"Purely for security reasons."

I didn't know what they'd told Binnie. It was certain to have borne no relation to the truth, but whatever it was I'd only find out by asking her when I saw her. I had a feeling I was being set up for a sucker punch and I didn't care for it.

"No," I said. "Sorry. After all I haven't done brilliantly so far, have I? I didn't want to get involved in the intelligence side of this in the first place, as I thought I made clear. And the more I see of it the more I'm convinced that I was too bloody right."

Greve-Gillett stuffed away the last of his papers and zipped the case shut.

"It is a matter of some importance, you know," he said. "I feel I should stress that. One hesitates to use the phrase 'national interest,' but . . ."

"National interest, my left knee," I said. "If I thought this was part of a shooting war, I'd climb into my little tin hat and boots all right." I looked over towards Sloane. "But you know what I think?" I told him. "I think you, Mr. Sloane, are just having a private game of Grandmothers Footsteps with Kiess and his bunch of trigger-happy little goons, and as far as I'm concerned you can find yourself another boy. Besides," I turned back to Christopher Greve-Gillett again, "if I get all bent, who's going to carry out your next lot of Flittermouse Trials?"

He stood up.

"Very well," he said. He looked around with the air of a chairman winding up an inconclusive committee meeting. "I think that we all owe Dr. Yeoman our thanks for his help so far."

"Just a moment," said Driver. He turned to me. The charm came on like a quartz-iodine lamp. "We'd still be very grateful if you'd come along to the next lot of trial flights, just as an observer."

"All right," I said cautiously. "But why?"

"Well, after all you're the chap who knows most about the control side of Tree Frog, aren't you?" he said. I didn't think so, it seemed to me that several dozen people who had actually designed and built the thing knew a good deal more, but I didn't say so. "It's based on your work," said Driver, "and you've seen the plane itself. What about taking a look at the ground support system in action as well? There's probably a lot of help you could give us there."

"So that next time I run into Kiess and Maxius I can tell them all about that too?" I asked. "It's the only thing so far I haven't been able to assist them with."

"I don't think," said Driver carefully, "that any of us

would want you to be exposed to that sort of risk again. Don't worry."

I knew this was all a good bit of committee work. I knew he was probably quite happy to settle for my cooperation as an observer, it was probably all he wanted anyway and the tactics are well known.

"I'll come and watch," I said. "Where?"

"Sand and sun," said Driver. "You'll love it."

Later that night I was sure I'd got the whole thing worked out. I was in a small bedroom with a steel locker at the top of the house, just above my temporary office. The plane was due to leave at seven the next morning, but I couldn't sleep.

I didn't know where they'd sent Binnie to keep her out of the way, but they'd solved the knotty problem of what to do with me. By getting me to act as trials observer, Driver had put me under wraps for the moment. What his reasons were for doing so I couldn't guess, but it seemed reasonable that he wouldn't want me telling everybody what the weather was like in Austria for a bit.

About two o'clock I remembered there was still a piece missing. I got out of bed and dressed.

Downstairs, there was a line of light showing under the door of Driver's office, and when I pushed it gently it swung open.

They were playing chess. Sloane didn't look up. I would never know about Sloane, and I suppose it didn't matter. He was probably front man for an enormous computer buried deep under Whitehall. I had the feeling that what was happening now had already happened long ago in Sloane's mind and there was nothing I could do about it.

Driver saw me and came to the door. He must have been something of a mind reader himself, because he gave me no chance to speak.

"Sorry about all that unpleasant business in Vienna," he said. "We should have known they wanted to talk to you pretty badly, of course."

"How?"

"Well, there was that affair of your car crash, wasn't there?" he said. "The intention was probably to get hold of you then, don't you think? It would be a convenient way of doing it. Hospital and all that, you know."

"A bit risky, though," I said. "They took much better care of me in Vienna. Besides, I don't see Michael in his commando suit and carrying his tiny popgun as part of the English countryside."

"It wouldn't have to be him, would it?"

"I thought perhaps it was you," I said unpleasantly.

"My dear chap." It was about the twentieth time he'd said it since I came back. "You mustn't think we're absolute blackguards. You really mustn't."

"I'll try to bear it in mind."

"Was there something you wanted?"

"Not now," I said. Behind Driver's back, Sloane moved a piece with great care and precision. I couldn't see what move he'd made, I was too far away.

Nineteen

AL QARIF did not exist until a few years ago, when someone bored a hole deep down into the crust of the desert and found water. Man exists at Al Qarif as a mosquito exists, sucking life through a tiny puncture in the skin of the Libyan Sahara. One day, any day—you can feel it—the Sahara will shrug and the mosquito will no longer be there. The puncture will heal over and man will be forgotten, as he has been countless times before.

We touched down in our Twin Pioneer at the tail end of a dust storm. The wheels spurted long plumes of sand, bit through to the buried surface of the landing strip, and the plane slewed from side to side as it chewed its way to rest in 150 yards. We climbed out, coughing our lungs clear, into a temperature of 110 degrees and a humidity of nothing at all.

The first thing you learn is to keep your mouth shut. If you don't, the air you breathe rips the lining of your mouth and throat away like a rasp. Driver wore a pith helmet. Nobody knew where he'd got hold of it. Perhaps he was an empire-builder in the days when only mad dogs and Englishmen went out in the midday sun. I explained to him very carefully that there is no such thing as sunstroke and that you can get heat-stroke, which is entirely different in conception, whether or not your head is covered, but of course he merely thanked me and retained the helmet throughout.

Inside the Mess Hut it was cooler. We were given hot sweet tea and biscuits. The tea tasted faintly of sulphur and washing soda, but I got used to it. I left Driver, Chapman and Andy Dylan talking to the C.O., a morose wing commander called Baker, and looked out of the window.

Outside the air changed from reddish brown to a glaring white as the dust settled. The wind still blew fitfully, sweeping the sand on the airstrip into miniature dunes before scouring it clean. Al Qarif was made largely of plastic, which gave it an even more temporary feel. The technical equipment huts were double-skinned plastic on cement frames. Even the strip itself was a mixture of PVC and concrete, because the tarmac would have softened in the sun and plain cement would have cracked in the alternate heat and cold of the desert day and night.

At the far end of the strip, a brilliantly white hemisphere curved against the sky. It must be the radome. Men walked about in shorts and bleached blue shirts, trying to look military.

I turned away into the dimness of the hut and hoped we wouldn't be here too long. If you don't like the desert it's hell and if you stay there too long it stops being hell and starts to grip your mind and soul and after that everywhere else is hell instead, so they said. I didn't know the desert and I was quite happy to keep things on that footing. Driver, Chapman and Andy were immersed in conversation at the other side of the hut, so I put my sunglasses back on and headed for the door. As I opened it a hand fell on my shoulder and Wing Commander Baker spoke.

"Care to take a look around, Dr. Yeoman?" he asked.

We went out into the glare.

"How long have you been here?" I asked.

"Eleven months," he said. "It's a fifteen month tour. Over the hump." Baker tended to talk as though he'd been seconded to some outpost on the Northwest Frontier for life. We were walking slowly around the camp, and every now and again he would go over to a hut or a tent and give it a rapid examination, as though he thought it might be a mirage and would disappear if he didn't keep checking that everything was still there.

"I don't suppose it's a popular posting," I said.

"Depends on your point of view. At least I've never had an A.O.C.'s inspection. Don't suppose I ever shall," he said.

We reached the radome. It was smaller than I'd imagined, seeing it from a distance, but it still seemed to dominate the camp. Perhaps it was thirty feet across. I rapped on it experimentally.

"Expanded plastic," said Baker. "Supposed to stay cool."

"And doesn't it?" I asked.

"No, not really," he said. "Just like all the other bright ideas around here. Nearly works but not quite. Not that it matters all that much now. Do most of our exercises at night and all the chaps wear flying jackets. Brass monkey work at night, I can tell you. Sorry you can't go inside until I've been told the form officially."

I studied him. He was scanning the sky with his hand

shading his forehead as though he were wondering if it would rain. He was one of those people who never go brown no matter how long they stay in the sun, but he wasn't red either. Despite his remittance-man air, he was the best possible man to have in charge of a place like this. Too tight a hand, and somebody would probably go amuck with a bayonet one hot day. Too loose, and everyone would be lying about swigging compass fluid and going native.

"What's that block over there?" I asked.

He followed my finger. At the far end of the landing strip, beyond the tarpaulined shapes of three or four aircraft, was a long, low building with what looked like an auxiliary power plant stuck on the end of it as an afterthought.

"That's for the Yanks," said Baker. "Nobody there at the moment, they come and go as they see fit. I think they're due in tonight." He sounded vaguely censorious, as though the Americans were, like locusts, a fact of life which had to be endured.

"What on earth are the Americans doing here?" I asked.

"God knows," said Baker moodily. "They've got the lot, of course. Air conditioning's a hundred percent better than ours. One transport plane per man, just about, full of deep-frozen T-bone steaks I suppose. Haven't had one here since February, though I must admit he was a nice enough chap to have around. Geologist."

"Oil?" It seemed likely.

"Oil, uranium, I don't know," he said. "What they'd do if they found anything is something else again. We're five hundred miles from anywhere."

I wondered if Driver knew about the Americans. He must

have. It surprised me. I knew they had an air base at Wheelus Field by Tripoli, but what were they attached to Al Qarif for? Drinking water, just like us, probably. In the desert, water is the source and explanation of all sorts of unlikely circumstances.

It was late afternoon, and the air was getting fractionally cooler. I looked outwards, past the unfenced perimeter where the camp blended into the bare desert beyond, across broken rock and blackened, oxidized sandy slopes. There was still just enough haze in the air to limit vision before the horizon. There was an impression of being closed in; that we were in the hollow of a hand, brown and yellow, orange and gray, a hand which could close on us if it chose to do so. Over to the south and west I could barely see the tops of a tall rock escarpment, perhaps the edge of the Tibesti, the high plateau which juts like a wart out of French Equatorial Africa.

Five hundred miles from anywhere, Baker said. I turned my head, and found that he was walking away towards the airstrip, his head down.

Five hundred miles. All right. So they could fly Tree Frog around to their hearts' content without disturbing the neighbors.

But so they could if they took it to Woomera instead. And the maintenance and fueling problems would be far easier to solve in Australia. So why set up shop here?

The wing commander was striding on towards the line of parked aircraft, cowled and hooded against the blowing sand. I plodded after him, scuffing dust over my toecaps.

"There's your baby," said Baker. "In there." The hut he was pointing at was exactly like all the others, except that it was plastered with notices saying KEEP OUT and EXPLOSIVE FUEL.

Tree Frog itself burned high-flash kerosene, but there was a small high-output power plant just forward of wing-center; a tiny jewel of a generator which burned, for a short hundred second burst, an oxidant-propellant mixture which spun a turbine shaft. I'd seen it at Monkham Manor. A self-contained short-life power plant is often the best answer if you want a lot of power for a small space of time, as Tree Frog did when it landed. Such a plant weighs far less than its equivalent in batteries, and at the same time it avoids the problems of auxiliary power takeoff from the main turbine, which in any case may not be running by then.

Baker was looking at me expectantly. Did he think I was going to hurl myself forward and embrace Tree Frog in a blaze of parental fervor, or what?

"Not my baby," I said. "I don't care if you let it go at forty thousand feet and it just drops like a stone."

He looked as though I'd struck him a mortal blow.

"But I understood you practically designed the control system from the floor up," he said.

"Who told you?"

"Your crew of Intelligence wallahs," he said.

"Wrong again," I said. "If Tree Frog is supposed to be my baby then I'm an unnatural parent. And the Intelligence wallahs aren't anything to do with me either, and I'm beginning to get good and fed up with people assuming they are. Okay?"

I knew what had happened. Driver had wished an unknown civilian on him. Me. Driver had also known he wouldn't like the idea one bit, especially not in the middle of the desert, so Seeker had given me an official build-up as the single-handed creator of Tree Frog. No doubt they'd presented me as an eccentric thrown in for good measure. That sort of thing would be practically a routine operation for Seeker.

Now I could see Baker turning over ideas in his mind, such as having an armed guard assigned to me as permanent escort for instance. I didn't want him to get ulcers.

"It's okay," I said. "Just kidding."

I found that they had given me a hut entirely to myself. I used the rationed jugful of water supplied to wash my face and neck, and changed my shirt. Then I walked across to the hut next door, hoping I'd find Andy Dylan. As I came in, I saw a familiar figure on the nearest bed. It was Flight Sergeant Kelsey, Ph.D.

"Hello, Kel," I said.

He looked up. He seemed embarrassed to see me for some reason.

"Hello," he said. He stood up. "Nice to see you here. Have you had a shufti at all you want yet?"

"I'd like to take a long hard look around the inside of that radome," I told him, "but otherwise yes, thanks."

"Good, good," said Kelsey. He still seemed distracted, as though he wasn't sure he ought to be seen talking to me, though he was cheerful enough. I wondered if he'd heard what had been going on since I visited Monkham Manor. Maybe he regarded Tree Frog with all the parental affection I'd failed to show Wing Commander Baker. If it had got back to him that I had told the opposition all about it, maybe he thought I'd sold them all down the river. I didn't know, and he was no help.

"Well, see you," he said. He left the hut and went out into the short tropical evening.

"What was all that about?" I asked Andy. He swung off his bed and went over to the mirror.

"All what about?"

"Kelsey."

Andy adjusted his precision-folded open shirt.

"Is there something wrong with him?" he asked.

"Yes," I said. "He's giving me the civilian nuthead treatment, only he's too polite to go the whole hog."

He came over and steered me towards the door.

"Let's go and grab some chow," he said. "I think you're getting persecution mania."

"It's not that," I told him. "It's just that everybody keeps on persecuting me."

Twenty

THE desert night is everything they tell you it is. Hard and brittle as tempered steel and spread with impossible thousands of stars. I looked back and saw the lights of Al Qarif below and behind me, a bare half-mile away, but I still felt alone. I needed to be.

The air was getting cold, but the rocks I walked over still held some of the day's heat. I stopped and lay down, turning onto my back. I hoped that if I stayed there long enough my brain would become as clear as the sky above me.

After ten minutes there was a growing rumble of aircraft engines to the north. I lay still, looking upwards, while a twin-engined transport roared overhead, a silhouette studded with navigation lights. It throttled back to a mutter, and sank slanting to the ground. I could hear the sharp squeal of its tires as it touched down on the strip. The Americans and their deep-frozen T-bone steak, no doubt.

Air travel has shrunk the world all right. Vienna was two thousand miles away, London two and a half.

It would be nice to say that I'd been dragged unwillingly

all that distance, that I'd been tricked into everything, that none of this was my own choosing except that I could have refused, I suppose, when they offered me an office at Seeker. But there was more to it than that.

Who said "curiosity killed the cat?" Pzenica, of course, I remembered now.

I knew there was something terribly phony about Tree Frog, and it was curiosity, the urge to find out for my own personal satisfaction just exactly what was phony about it, which had almost killed me twice already and might, for all I knew, kill me yet.

Just so long as it was clear in my mind. I'd still go on bellyaching if Driver or anyone else tried to push me around the board, but I couldn't afford to fool myself.

I closed my eyes.

When I opened them again, I thought I'd slipped gear, into a world where you rubbed lamps and genies appeared. A man was looking down at me. He was well over six feet tall, and he wore a white shirt and *seroual*, the flowing, black trousers of the desert with the white pattern down one side. His head was turbaned, and he carried a short sword at his waist and a dagger strapped to his upper arm. He had stepped straight from the Arabian Nights.

I sat up slowly. I knew little about protocol in the Sahara, except that it would be unwise at most, impolite at the least, to move in a hurry. He watched me steadily.

He was, I knew, a Tarqui, one of the Forgotten People of Allah, the Twarek. The French, who fought against them for so many years, call them the Touareg. I was surprised to see his face uncovered, for usually all you see of the Tarqui is his eyes. I nodded at him, feeling a fool.

"Hi, Giles," said someone behind me. I recognized Yancy's voice and turned.

"I might have known it would be you," I said.

"Who else?" asked Yancy. He was, I saw, dressed in similar clothes to the Tarqui. It is only the British who have a mania for displaying the kneecaps nowadays.

"This is Mohammed Jalil al Murzuq. He drives for me," said Yancy. "If it's any easier, he doesn't mind being called Jeep. Okay?"

I scrambled ungracefully to my feet. Jeep even managed a slight smile. I felt more than ever like an ill-mannered idiot. I'd met the Touareg only once before when I was in Morocco; they have an unfailing air of aristocracy, even in the city, which is far from being their element. Here in the desert, that section of the world's surface which belonged exclusively to him and his people, he was overwhelming. I felt as though I'd been camping out in the middle of his living room carpet. He held out his hand, since I was his guest.

"Jeep," he said.

I told him my name. He inclined his head and walked away a few paces. I could see the lights of the camp behind him. We were, all of us, his guests. We kept our precarious hold on his land through his compliance and the will of Allah, *Inch' Allah.* I understood this now, and it helped the perspective view I took of myself and of Tree Frog.

"A good guy to have around," said Yancy. "If I said I'd

be lost without him, it'd be a sick joke. You can lose yourself just like that"—he snapped his fingers—"out here."

"I'm not going far," I said. "Just what the hell are you doing here?"

"U.S.A.F. liaison," he said. "What do you think I'm doing?"

"Does Driver know that's what you're here for?"

"Sure he does."

It fitted in with Yancy's curiosity about crashed drones and other things in Vienna. By right I ought to have been asking him a couple of questions about his trip to the airport with Binnie, but I left it for the moment. He held out a packet of cigarettes, and gave one to Jeep.

"Nice place, this, though," he said, looking around. "Not that I'd bring the kids. Like the joke says, it's a long way from the sea."

"How did you know I was here?" I asked.

"Old man Driver said you were on the field. I called in your hut but you weren't anywhere around. Jeep spotted you up here."

I didn't take him up on it. I could believe it.

"Well, now," said Yancy. "I hear you've been in all sorts of trouble."

"So you came flying all the way out here to see if you could help."

He grinned. "Don't think I'm being nosy," he said. "Only I did hear that the boys over the other side of the palisade gave you a tough time."

"Everyone's been giving me a tough time," I said. "Don't

you start, because I need that like I need an extra elbow."

"Not me. I'm your old friend, your old buddy, Cap'n Yancy Brightwell, remember?"

"Okay," I said.

"They can be tough when they try. Even when they aren't trying, they can be tough," he said. "I know that."

"Not only that," I told him, "but through some administrative cock-up which I don't even have to try to explain to you, they also had hold of my girl. As no doubt you know. And in the U.K. we don't stand for people even thinking of getting tough with our girls. You may have heard."

"Not unless you're doing it yourselves. Yes, I did hear tell," said Yancy. He shifted his cigarette. "I'm sorry about that," he went on. "I should have stayed with her until her flight left, I guess. I can see it must have put you on the spot."

"That's right, it did," I said. "Leave it there." He nodded. "There are a couple of things I could do with your telling me, if it comes to that," I went on.

"Such as?"

"Was that plane you came in on really full of deep-frozen steaks? Baker reckons so."

"Nah," said Yancy. "Freeze-dried. Everything freeze-dried, it's the new word from the logistics men. Freeze-dried steak we've got, yes, freeze-dried waffles and corn syrup, freeze-dried Original Old Creole Chicken Gumbo. Even freeze-dried ice cream. Only thing the logistics boys didn't figure is there's no water to add to the damn stuff, but you can't win them all. What did you have?"

"Fried eggs, sausages and chips," I told him. "That's why

our morale is so high. Also why you get fat and we don't."

"Nobody gets fat in the desert," he said. He nodded towards Jeep. "Ask him. What else did you want to know?"

"Why you're here at all," I said. "If we were in England there'd be wire all round us with big signs saying, Keep Out, This Means Yanks. How come we're such buddies with you out here?"

He thought it over for a minute or two while he finished his cigarette and field-stripped the butt.

"It was a deal," he said. "Nothing was signed, but that's what it amounts to."

"It sounds familiar," I said. "Is Driver happy about it?"

"He's not jumping for joy."

"Good," I said. "If he was, then I'd say you had the sticky end. What did you do, threaten to break off diplomatic relations?"

"Easier than that," said Yancy. "See, the Libyan Government allows both the British and the Americans to maintain military installations on its territory. By the same token, you can hardly stop us overflying, can you?"

"Even if we wanted to," I said.

"Of course. Of course. We're allies, aren't we?" said Yancy. He grinned. "Anyway, since you can't stop us looking, I suppose some bright boy decided you might as well ask us in. That way you can keep an eye on us, is the idea."

"So you sit in your air-conditioned hut and watch us fly things around?" I asked.

"That's right," he said. "Unless somebody forgets to lock up and I get a good look round that radar installation."

You and me both," I told him. "If you get in there first, you might tell me how it looks."

"I'll send you a copy of my evaluation for U. S. Air Force Intelligence when I've written it up," he promised. Behind us, Jeep stood up silently. "Come on back to American territory," said Yancy, "and I'll stand you a genuine freeze-dried Pilsener beer. How about that?"

Twenty-One

As it happened I got into the radome the next morning. Wing Commander Baker liked having me around even less than he liked Yancy, but he'd done his checking higher up the line. At half past six Andy Dylan hauled me out of bed and at five to seven I was escorted by Driver over to the plastic bubble. There were no security guards, which made sense because there wasn't anywhere to run to from Al Qarif.

They left me to look around for myself. I pulled the door to behind me and shut out the Sahara. In here it was like being in an aquarium.

Above me was the aerial array, directly underneath the hemispherical roof itself. One rotating parabolic reflector. One vertical rocking scanner. One small directional dish which was motionless at the moment and I guess was servo-driven. I couldn't see any aerials for the remote control system unless the small dish itself was part of it.

The dome hummed and throbbed with power. Power for the scanners and motors, power running in h.f. waveguides, power for cooling and power for the computing system. It was cool and dark. We might have been anywhere in the world. There were no windows, and the quiet curve of the dome vanished overhead in the greenish twilight sprayed from concealed lamps.

I circled along the outer wall of the dome, around the central mass of computers and control gear, cross-hatched with narrow access aisles. There was no operator on duty and when I came to the radar watch area there was no one there. The bright scanning sweep swung around the orange tube face of the monitor like the seconds hand of a stopwatch. I can never stand by a radarscope for long without recalling the Rubaiyat; the moving Finger writes. Out here it seemed more appropriate than ever.

Kelsey was in one of the aisles, head and shoulders immersed in disemboweled racks of electronic gear. I thought of tapping him on the shoulder, but I moved on. Instead I moved another quarter circle around the circumference of the dome and squatted beside a corporal technician who was whistling a tune from *West Side Story*. I told him who I was and what I was doing here and he put down his Avo for a minute.

"Oh, yeah?" he said. "Owen. You the doc they've been telling us about then?"

"Depends what they've been telling you," I said.

"You're on the flying end, Kelsey said."

It seemed a fairly accurate way of describing things, for a change.

"You could say that. How does the equipment stand up to things in here?" I asked him.

"It's a right bastard," said Corporal Technician Owen succinctly. "Can't keep the bastard sand out. Can't use any oil or it's worse. See that?" He tapped the next rack along the aisle with the handle of an insulated screwdriver. "Hundred and twenty-two semiconductors in there, all radiating heat like bastard bonfires. What's the time?"

"Ten past seven," I said.

"Right. Ten past seven. By twelve noon," said Owen, getting into his stride, "it'll be like a bloody oven in here, man. All those transistors are supposed to run cool, but they don't because the air's hotter than they are. What are we supposed to do, blow on them? This rig is operational two percent of the time and u.s. the rest, and if I wasn't here it'd fall to bits inside a minute. Otherwise it's not bad."

I went back and looked at the radar screen.

"It's operational now," I pointed out.

"Oh sure. Early morning's it's fine."

I realized that it was probably fine most of the time when you got down to cases. Technicians, like camel drivers, make a habit of reviling their equipment. It's just one of those things.

"What's the range of this set?" I asked him.

"Four hundred miles. When it's in a good temper."

I looked at the screen again. There was an echo out at seventy miles if this was the case, closing on center from about three twenty degrees or so. I told him.

"Transport," he said. "I think the birdmen are due in this morning."

"The launch aircrew? For the drone?"

"That's right, doc."

"How many flight trials have you done already?" I asked him.

"On Tree Frog? Six weeks with the Mark One before those silly bastards took it back home and dropped it in the drink. Nothing with the Mark Two, not yet."

"Tell me how the system works," I said. I might just as well check that my guesses had come out right. He lumbered over to where I stood at the set.

"Easy. This here," he tapped the face of the tube, "is ordinary P.P.I. approach radar. That gives you your range and bearing. All right then. Say that echo's your drone up there," he tapped the tube face again over the single echo visible, "then you got your vertical scan radar for altitude. The echoes from both sets are shoved into that computer over there," he sighted along his screwdriver like a pistol, "and the output from the computer drives your radio control aerial direct so you're laughing kitbags. Okay?"

"Okay," I said.

"Right, well, that's it, isn't it? Your radar homes your control beam and keeps it aimed at the bastard drone automatically. I don't know about the actual control end, that's nothing to do with me."

It all sounded plausible, and I was sure it worked at close range. But not at anything over, say, fifty miles. Not with this equipment. I knew it, Driver knew it, Maxius knew it. Kiess wasn't sure about it, but then he wasn't a technician, or at least not in this line of work anyway.

"How well does it do the job?" I asked Owen. "Does it actually stay locked onto the drone in flight?"

"Sometimes it does," said Owen.

"All the time, when we've ironed out the snags. You wait and see," said Driver over my shoulder. Chapman was on the other side of me. It looked as though they'd decided to break things up. Chapman surveyed me over his glasses in a vaguely benevolent academic way.

"That's right," said Chapman. "That's what we're here for. To iron out the snags." He bent forward and scrutinized the radar screen. The single blip of the transport had crept in to about twenty-five miles range by now and was approaching on each sweep of the scanner, leaving behind it a trail of fading ghost images from previous sweeps. Chapman looked fascinated, as though he'd never seen one before in his life.

He and Driver, I realized, were two halves of the same individual, locked together in some mysterious symbiosis. Driver was the man of action, or at least that was the way he pushed himself across at the rest of the world, and Chapman was the withdrawn, intellectual don. He didn't talk as much as Driver, but then he didn't have to. Perhaps he'd heard the rhyme about the wise old owl who sat on an oak. And over and above the two of them sat Sloane. The remote manipulator, the strategist. At the beginning of the affair, I could see, Sloane had lifted his head and said, "This is what I want done." And Chapman had worked out the ways and means of doing it, and Driver had translated those ways and means into action.

A nice, smooth, efficient team. Not a committee, a team, everyone with his own part. It is only nice, smooth, efficient teams which survive in the world of government departments without falling apart or fossilizing.

The only thing wrong was that I came under the heading of Ways and Means, and I wasn't sure I liked it.

"And the best of luck," I said to Chapman.

I picked up smooth pebbles, one by one, and threw them into the night. Mohammed Jalil al Murzuq sat still, only his eyes moving slightly at the faint click as each one landed. He was dressed in the style of his own people now, in the long robes and the veil, the *litham*, drawn across his face. He looked incongruous at the wheel of the jeep which gave him his nickname. But then we looked incongruous in his desert.

"Come on, Giles boy," said Yancy. "You going to make up your mind or not? It's fair trade."

"I haven't been in the trading game that long," I said.

"Okay," he said peaceably. "I'll throw my information in for free. No strings."

"All right," I said. "I'm probably being a sucker again, but you can't pick up the rules without playing a couple of hands."

"That's the spirit," said Yancy. We walked over to the jeep. I got in beside Mohammed and Yancy piled into the back, wedging himself between four petrol cans. He touched Mohammed on the shoulder.

"Let's go," he said.

Mohammed fired the motor. I looked over towards the camp, a glowing ring of light in the darkness half a mile away. We rolled away, the jeep's motor snarling gently across the indigo sands.

Twenty-Two

I LOOKED out ahead and tried to see beyond the dim pool of yellow where the single headlamp beam lit the surface in front of us, but I couldn't make anything out. Mohammed wasn't driving by the headlamp anyway, it was probably just a nuisance to him. He drove at a steady forty and it was like being on a roller coaster and not being able to tell if the track was chopped off short ten yards ahead of you.

Yancy crammed his cap down over his eyes in the back of the jeep.

"How far are we supposed to be going?" I asked him. He spread his hands and then jerked his thumb at Mohammed.

"Try it on him," he said.

"How far?" I asked.

"*Beit,*" said Mohammed. His eyes never left the ground twenty yards beyond the glare of the headlamp.

"Long way," Yancy translated helpfully. "Don't worry. They're going to have your stripes tomorrow anyway, for undue fraternization. So relax."

We hit a flat rock and one side of the jeep bounced two feet into the air. Yancy cursed the petrol cans fluently and fought himself back into something approaching a comfortable position again.

"Worse than camels," he said. "Hey, Jeep, knock it off, will you?"

Mohammed paid no attention whatever. A mile or so farther on he eased his foot off the throttle fractionally, but it was only to swerve to the right. I could still see very little of the terrain, but what I could see looked exactly the same in every direction to me. Mohammed had evidently reached a fork in some mental road of his own which he could see perfectly well.

"How about it, then, Giles?" said Yancy. "You going to tell Uncle all about it or are you still playing British?"

"That radome is covered by the Official Secrets Act," I told him.

"You don't say."

"They wouldn't even let me in before Baker had got clearance from the Prime Minister," I said. "What do you think, I'm going to draw you a blueprint?"

"I hope it was worth it," said Yancy. "Now come on. You can't figure out what's going on by yourself. Nor can I if it comes to that. But we might get a toe-hold on it if we put our heads together."

I didn't answer.

"Have it your way," he said.

An hour and a half later we were in the middle of nowhere at all. Coming from nowhere and headed towards nowhere. Mohammed switched the engine off and coasted to a standstill without using the brakes. He flicked off the lights and we got out.

Except that there was no camp, we could have been just where we started out from. There was nothing at all to distinguish this particular spot in the desert from any other.

One thinks of the Sahara as entirely covered with sand dunes. It isn't. It's just that the first bits the tourist sees when approaching from the more popular bits of the North African coast are liable to be the Great Western Erg or the Great Eastern Erg. There was plenty of sand here all right, but it was mostly spread out in flat plains. The most constant feature was rock. Loose rock, rock scoured and filed into fantastic cones and pinnacles by centuries of desert wind.

I looked at my watch. Just after midnight. It was cold and empty and we lit cigarettes for reassurance.

"Okay," said Yancy. "Let me guess. I know the state of the art as well as you do and I know radar and guidance from here to gone and back. That's a pretty small installation you've got at Al Qarif."

I nodded. I could see it coming a mile off.

"I don't mean just in comparison with what we've got back home, where everybody knows we build everything bigger and better than you do. I've seen blisters that big on the top of ham shacks, and so have you."

He slapped his hands thoughtfully on the side of the jeep. "So either you've got something in there that's so revolutionary we'd better buy it off you quick or else you haven't, in which case I don't know what all the fuss is about. Come to think of it, your power trucks don't have all that helluva capacity either. So I say you're just doing ordinary overhead field trials with limited radio guidance equipment and the hell with Driver and the rest of the circus. Except for one thing."

"What thing?"

Yancy didn't answer. I didn't push it.

All of a sudden I began to get very tired of Driver and Chapman. With monotonous regularity, everybody with the slightest technical knowledge, myself included, had taken a look at Tree Frog and given a great big horse laugh.

It would be nice to think we were all wrong. It would be nice to think that, as Yancy implied, underneath all that ordinary radar gear lay the most stupendous advance in the history of remote-controlled flight. All in a little black box under the radar operator's chair and powered by the batteries from somebody's transistor set. The trouble is, that isn't the way life works, not in electronics anyway.

But I began, seriously, to think that it might be the only explanation.

Yancy stubbed out his cigarette on the tire of the jeep.

"Right, men," he said. "A little walk." Mohammed started off, leaving the jeep just where it was. We followed. An awful lot of people had fouled me up in the last few weeks, and maybe this was all part of the act, but there wasn't anything I could do about it if so.

Yancy's little walk was a forty-minute route march, and my only consolation was that he was in far worse shape than I. Some of the time it was rock underfoot, but more often it was like thrashing through a snowdrift. The fine sand rose over my ankles and sifted down into the soles of my boots, and Mohammed moved ahead of me like a ghost.

He signaled us to stop. I thought we might be going to take a breather, but instead we spent the next ten minutes crawling up and over a low ridge of rock, and when we got to the top I could see why. Sound travels a long way across the desert, and even though we'd left the jeep a long way behind they might still have heard us.

It looked like a smallish Touareg encampment. On the other side of the hollow beneath us I could see the glint of water in a rock pool. Between it and our ridge were six or seven tents, huddled low against the sides of the hollow in a haphazard ring. A man was sitting by the *guelta,* his outline reflected in the water surface. He seemed to be holding a rifle, but it was difficult to tell from this distance. Mohammed put a hand on my sleeve and Yancy nodded slightly in benediction as I slid down the reverse of the ridge behind him, pulling myself along by my elbows. It was all very well, but I didn't know what the penalty was for being caught.

The ridge sloped steeply down and then dropped about two feet to the sand. Mohammed rolled the last six inches or so and then whipped over the rock edge like a snake. I was a good deal more clumsy and I thought I'd made enough noise to wake the dead. We lay in the angle of the rock for what seemed like an hour before Mohammed would move.

Just as I was beginning to send down roots he half rose and ran at a crouch towards the nearest tent. I followed him, and he stopped me about five feet away from the tent wall. I wanted to get under cover against the tent but instead he scraped at the sand in front of us for a few seconds and then guided my hand into the shallow, saucerlike depression he'd made. I felt something half-buried and lifted it with my fingers. It was a power cable.

The low side walls of the tent were made of rugs, leaning against the skin rock from inside. About halfway along the back wall there was a tiny slit of light showing. He pushed the tip of a finger into it, to widen it, motioning me to look through, and I lay in the sand and squinted.

He gave me ten seconds and then allowed the slit to close. Then we crawled back all the way we'd come. I thought we must have left a trail in the sand as big as a six-lane highway, at least I must have done, but Mohammed didn't seem bothered.

When we got back again to the top of the ridge where Yancy was waiting, I saw that the sentry was still sitting by the *guelta* in the same attitude, and I realized we could only have taken about five minutes for the whole operation. My shirt was sticking to my back, but it was worth it. Domestic utensils among the Touareg do not, presumably, include even smallish ships' radar installations. I wouldn't have sworn to the type, not in the ten seconds Mohammed had given me. It might even have been a re-jigged airborne radar set. I don't know.

Yancy was still looking smug when we got back to the jeep.

"Had to show you, or you'd have said I was kidding," he said.

"I don't know," I told him. "It's getting so's I'll believe almost anything these days."

Mohammed was sitting at the wheel again. It was nothing to do with him.

"I think they made an error setting up at a water hole," said Yancy. "Somebody was bound to drop by sooner or later. It could be they don't care. They may not be here for long. When's the first test flight?"

"Tomorrow night," I said.

"What's the flight plan? Or is that covered by the Official Secrets Act too?"

"Nobody's told me," I said. "We can all find out at the briefing tomorrow."

"You don't sound wildly excited at the prospect."

"I'm not," I said.

"Well," said Yancy, "somebody's excited enough to set up a little tiny radar station all on its own in the middle of the desert, just to see what goes on. And that's the only thing that makes me want to stick around. I'd like to see what goes on, too."

I got back into the jeep.

"I hope nobody gets disappointed," I said.

Twenty-Three

At five the next afternoon, give or take ten minutes or so, we were packing the aisles for Group Captain Nockolds' briefing session. I'd only been out of bed for an hour, after last night's exercise, and the place seemed to have filled up during the day. Several more aircraft had arrived, and what with air crew, ground crews, radar operating crews, maintenance crews, orderlies, clerks, policemen and cooks Al Qarif was getting to look like the Golden Mile.

I slid into an empty chair beside Yancy, who was craning out of the window. Somewhere out of vision but not sound, a group of indefatigable cretins were playing cricket and he could hardly believe it was true. I could hardly believe it myself, except that I knew the dogged persistence with which Sports Afternoon is perpetuated all over the world. It was well over a hundred inside here, even with Baker's joke air conditioning, and I felt as though I'd been for a quick roll in fish glue. Yancy, I noticed, looked crisp and uncreasable.

"Hi," he said.

"How do you do it?" I asked him. "We used to have the monopoly on the frosted empire-builder look."

"Easy, I keep my shorts in the freezer," he said. "It's a little idea I picked up on the side from my wife. Where were you all day?"

"In bed," I said.

Those of us who could be spared from the serious business of outdoor sports were beginning to form up in competitive teams in here, I saw. Royal Air Force, Monkham Manor, was represented by Nockolds himself and Kelsey, who sat alone at one end of the front row of chairs. The home side was fielding Wing Commander Baker, an Operations Intelligence officer with a sandy mustache called Hendrickson and a group of radar whiz kids of whom I only recognized Corporal Technician Owen. Over by the stove, Driver, Andy Dylan and Chapman muttered among themselves. They glanced occasionally in our direction and I felt the temperature drop every time they did so. Nobody had torn my stripes off, but there was an air of disapproval you could have sawn into chunks.

Nockolds stopped pacing up and down in front of the blackboard and faced front and center. The torrent of subdued conversation withered to a trickle and evaporated.

"What we're going to do tonight," said Nockolds, "is fly round in circles."

"Ever decreasing circles," said Kelsey. There was the sort of laughter you get at briefings.

"In point of fact, no," said Nockolds. "Ever increasing. But I'll get on to that in a minute or two. Some of us may not have had time to get acquainted with our launch crew." He nodded at another team, four this time, in the front row. They were dressed as though for space flight, probably in order to impress on us their ability actually to get off the ground. I couldn't see anything but the backs of their heads.

"Squadron Leader Bayliss," Nockolds went on briskly, "Flight Lieutenant Morris. Pilot and number two. Flight Lieutenant Brister, navigator. Flight Lieutenant Markham, electronics officer. Okay?"

I hadn't heard of any of them, and wondered if they'd been at Monkham Manor. From the back, they seemed to have identical close-cropped heads and carried bone-domes like cup finalists carry footballs. There was a brief murmur of welcome. Outside the window a sharp yelp of "Zat?" sounded, and at least a third of the heads in the room flicked towards the sound for an instant before going back to Nockolds.

"What about those crazy guys?" said Yancy.

"Take it back to your superior officers," I told him. "Britain's defenses are impregnable, except if anyone wants to invade they ought to pick about three on a Wednesday afternoon to send the first wave in and they'll walk it. The entire armed forces will be hitting, throwing or kicking balls around the place."

"Is that a fact?" said Yancy. "I'd have said Sunday."

"Don't be daft," I said. "On Sunday we're fully operational. It's the only way everybody can dodge church parades."

Nockolds pulled down the inevitable wall map and clipped it into place.

"You'll all have seen your detailed ops orders," he said. "This is just to present the allover picture again, okay? Now takeoff will be at twenty-two thirty hours, if the rain lets up, that is." There was another round of laughs. "Drop altitude will be eleven thousand feet. Kindly note, chaps, that there is a mountain down here, Emi Koussi," he hammered on the map, "whose peak is eleven thousand two hundred. So try not to get off course because we don't want the drone all bent. Since Emi Koussi is southwest of us and you'll be a hundred miles east, somebody will get a rollicking if anything of the sort happens. I'm just warning you. As soon as you've launched the drone, you'll return directly to base. I want you out of the sky fast. Some of us have difficulty seeing echoes on the P.P.I. and I don't want you in the way confusing us all. Check?"

Several voices answered "check." Notes were even being taken, I saw. Yancy dug me in the ribs.

"You tell anybody about our little friends in the desert yet?" he asked.

"No," I said. "I've only just got out of bed. What do you want me to do, get up and address the meeting?"

"Not right now," said Yancy. "Let's hear what the man's got to say first."

The heat was just beginning to lose the edge off its ferocity, but people were still mopping their necks. The feeling crowded in on me that we'd all gathered here, in the middle of Africa and a thousand miles for outside interference, to flight a local action, a tiny battle in war whose significance I couldn't yet see clearly. Outside, aircraft were being fueled and serviced, so that they could take part in an exercise which I'd have taken at face value if Seeker hadn't been around to muddy the water.

Fifty miles away in the Sahara, and for all I knew sprinkled around us like confetti, were men watching and listening with electronic eyes and ears. No shots were expected to be fired, but there was a battle on just the same.

"Those of you who were present at our Tree Frog Mark One trials here last year," said Nockolds, "will recall that those trials consisted of a series of short straight-line flights. Well, gentlemen, you'll be glad to hear that we can now fly in circles, at least we could in Lincolnshire last month. So unless we get a lot of sand in the works, that's what we're going to do now. Tree Frog will be tracked on ground radar and controlled by radio link from our seven-oh-four installation in the trailer right next to the radome out there. Right? Right. Flight path, as I've already indicated, will be a spiral, an outward spiral turning starboard. This means, believe it or not, that we shall be circling clockwise on the map. When we reach here," he tapped again, "and our turn radius is approximately thirty-five miles—"

"Approximately, nothing," said Kelsey.

"All right, Kel. Exactly. You're the boss inside that dome," said Nockolds. In point of fact there were two Technical Branch officers on Kelsey's left, but everyone knew what Nockolds meant. I began to feel sorry for Nockolds. Kelsey as *enfant terrible* at Monkham Manor was one thing, but he had to be brought out in public every now and again. I learned later that they spent a month every year trying to get Kelsey to go before a commissioning board so that it didn't look too much as though he was getting away with murder as a flight sergeant, but it never worked.

"When Tree Frog reaches here, *exactly*, weather and wind permitting."

"Okay," said Kelsey.

"She'll be brought in to land. You'll see that her glide path will bring her in about here, that is to say within five miles of Al Qarif, even if the radio control crew lose her at low altitude. We hope they won't, of course." He looked inquiringly at the radio control boys, who nodded with an air of being able to tackle anything.

"Right then," said Nockolds. "You've got your own detailed procedural breakdowns, so I think that's about all from me. Any questions?"

Yancy jabbed me in the ribs.

"Okay," he said. "Make your bid for glory."

Nockolds swung around, his hands behind his back.

"Yes," I said.

I stood up. I was all set to tell them that they were being watched all the time by low-power support radar and that they'd better think up some solid way of coping with the problem. Everybody turned to look at me, as everybody always does if only to see who's idiotic enough to ask questions at all. Out of the sea of faces, I only saw one man, the electronics officer from the launch crew. It was the first time I'd seen any of their faces. He was looking at me over the shoulder of his flying suit, with an interested expression.

"Yes?" Nockolds was being expansive, let's-be-nice-to-the-civilians. I hardly heard him.

"Nothing," I said. "Sorry. The answer is down here on the briefing summary."

"That's what it's for," said Nockolds cheerfully.

I sat down slowly.

"What's up?" asked Yancy.

I didn't answer. Nockolds had introduced the electronics officer as Flight Lieutenant Markham. But it wasn't the name I knew him by, and his face was burned onto my brain like a pokerwork motto. I didn't hear Nockolds winding up. The room was suddenly full of standing men, politely shuffling towards the exit doors. I fought my way over to the launch crew just as they were leaving by the door behind the rostrum.

"Phillips," I said.

I didn't expect him to answer, but I thought he might twitch. He didn't, of course. He walked out of the door and into the sunlight. It was like hailing somebody at a party and not being recognized, you feel suddenly as though you aren't there any more, that you have become invisible.

I followed him. The short bristles of his beard had gone. He put on his sunglasses, and still his face was exactly the same to me. I walked over to him, and he turned uncertainly to face me, swinging his helmet from his hand.

"You don't remember me," I said.

"I'm afraid not," said Flight Lieutenant Markham. "But hello anyway. You're the chap who did the control work on the drone, aren't you?"

"Yes," I said. "That's right."

He smiled. "She's a peach," he said. "A real peacheroo, believe you me. Don't worry, we'll take good care of her."

He nodded at me and then walked off to join the rest of the crew. Yancy came up behind me.

"You look as though you're seeing things," he said.

"I am," I told him. "The trouble is, they're going to say I've flipped my lid. Which I wouldn't mind so much, except I'd like to be sure I haven't."

I left him. When I looked back, he was standing with his hands in his pockets, staring after me. I knew what was going to happen when I told them, but I had to try anyway.

Twenty-Four

"THIS is going to sound crazy," I said, "but I can't think of any way to wrap it up for you. The electronics officer in your Tree Frog launch crew isn't on our side. He's on the away team."

"Oh yes?" said Driver. "Have a seat."

Chapman was opposite him. I sat down. They had a hut to themselves, which showed some presence of mind on Baker's part. With more presence of mind he'd have wired the place for sound, but he wasn't the type.

"When I last saw him, he was in my cell in that place in Austria," I said. "His name was Phillips and he wanted me to take him back home."

"I see," said Driver. He nodded.

"Look," I told him. "I'm not interested in this farcical bloody exercise of yours, but you asked me along and I'm doing my best for you. Now I know it sounds unlikely, but I dare say you've come across some fairly unlikely things in between chess games with Sloane. I'm telling you that one of your air crew is an enemy agent. Either because he always was or because Kiess had him around for a bit too long and persuaded him to change sides. And another thing, this station is under radar surveillance from at least one field post out there in the desert. More, for all I know, but I've seen one. Okay? Now I'll just let you get on with it by yourselves, shall I?"

There was a small stutter of coughing from the other chair. I'd forgotten about Dr. Chapman's irritating social habits.

"We did rather wonder where you'd got to last night," he said mildly. "Are we to take it that it was then you discovered this, ah, radar post?"

"That's right," I said.

"You were with Captain Brightwell."

"Yes," I said. I looked at Driver. He spread his hands in benediction.

"My dear chap, we've no objection," he said.

"Great," I said. "Now about Phillips."

"You mean Flight Lieutenant—" he appeared to search his memory for a moment—"Markham."

"For the sake of argument, yes," I said.

Chapman leaned back in his chair. "We've known Flight Lieutenant Markham for a very long time," he said. "His security rating is the same as your own. That applies of course to all air crew on this project."

I began to have a familiar feeling, as though I was slogging up the side of a sandhill, as Chapman got into his Senior Common Room stride.

"Your information about possible radar surveillance is most useful," he said. "Though of course we can't do anything about it. Not that we particularly want to." He glanced across at Driver, who nodded. "On the other hand, your suggestion about Markham . . ." He broke off and started a burst of coughing again.

"Is the product of a fevered brain," I finished for him. "All right, you don't have to spell it out for me."

"I don't mean to imply, er," said Chapman.

"No, but getting down to cases you're damned sure," I said.

"It really isn't on, old boy," said Driver.

"Ask him where he was a fortnight ago," I said. "If he was on his station I'll forget the whole thing. If nobody knows where he was, because he was having a nice long spot of leave on the continent—"

"I can see your point. We will, of course, check. But you would admit, wouldn't you, that you were in rather precarious mental balance during your own stay in Austria, weren't you? However temporary and for whatever good reasons. How often did you see this man Phillips?"

"Only once," I said.

"What build was he? How tall and so on?"

"I don't know," I said. "The only bit of him I saw properly was his face."

"How long after you'd been there?"

"You mean, how long had they been going over my cortex with the carbolic soap, I suppose," I said. "Sorry. I'd like to say it was right at the beginning and I was one hundred percent sound in mind, but I wasn't. On the other hand I wasn't seeing things, believe me."

Chapman settled still lower in his chair, looking relaxed and well balanced.

"In cases of this sort," he said, "as you yourself know quite well, there can be some very odd aftereffects."

"There can be, yes."

He leaned forward suddenly. "I suggest to you," he said, "and you know that I am not just arguing for the sake of it, that what you experienced just now in briefing was something akin to the phenomenon of *déja vu,* the illusion of having experienced something before. Common in structural brain damage, not so common in functional disturbances but perfectly possible. As you know."

I started to speak, but he went on firmly.

"It is a fact," he tapped the arm of his chair, "that Flight Lieutenant Markham is most unlikely to have been in Austria, or we'd know about it. If we haven't been told then we'll find out, of course, which of itself makes it even more unlikely. You can see that. If you're honest with yourself you must see it. You yourself have only just recovered, or perhaps I ought to say are still recovering, from a prolonged period of stress and possibly drugs. Are you prepared to swear that you did not, a few minutes ago, see Flight Lieutenant Markham as a man who *resembled* someone you saw while you were in a condition of extreme suggestibility? That your brain did not trick you, just for a moment, into believing you recognized him?"

He leaned back again. The trouble was that I knew he could be right. He wasn't, but he could be.

"Is that the way you see it too?" I asked Driver.

"One has to choose what seems to be the most likely of two explanations," he said. "Isn't that what you do in scientific research? Of course we'll act on what you've told us, and incidentally thank you very much indeed for taking the trouble to do so. But I wouldn't lose too much sleep about it if I were you."

It was the greased slide all right. I must say it was almost painless.

"I hope he doesn't just forget to switch on the works before he drops Tree Frog off," I said. "Or you may end up with an expensive crunch in the middle of nowhere. I don't know how you'd cope with my evidence at a Board of Inquiry if that happened, but I'm sure you'd come up with something."

I got up. Driver nodded brightly at me.

"I hope you'll be joining us at ten thirty," he said. "We're expected to put in an appearance at the tracking unit. And thank you once more for coming to us. We'll take the whole thing from here, don't you worry."

Now that it was dark outside, the station blazed like a goods yard. Engines were being run up to speed, the thin trails of oily smoke drifted across between the huts and the hangars. Jeeps drove here and there on life-and-death errands. I walked along the concrete apron which fronted all the quarters and looked over towards the airstrip, outlined in twin rows of pinpoint lights. Sound was being poured into the sky.

I finished a cigarette and walked towards my own hut. It was ten o'clock. Someone crossed the path in front of me, about twenty yards away, and I recognized Kelsey. He lifted a thumb at me.

"Good luck," he said. He vanished into the interstitial darkness, heading for the radome.

"Nothing to do with me," I called after him.

I went inside and sat back in one of the aluminum-framed armchairs. It was nothing to do with me. In half an hour I would go across to the tracking unit and watch them fly their spiral test course. If Phillips didn't hold everyone at gunpoint and fly the whole shooting match straight back to Red Square to collect his medals.

Outside the hut they were having trouble with an aircraft engine somewhere. I didn't even know what they were using to lift Tree Frog to launch altitude. If it was the Beverley they'd have to cut the cargo bay around a good deal to fit the drone underneath. Maybe they were trying out the Short Belfast, or could they put it down on a strip this size? I didn't know.

The air still blew slightly warm from the open door and smelt of aviation spirit and fried potatoes. I leaned back in the chair, and the man who was standing behind me crossed his forearms in front of my neck and took hold of my collar in the scissored carotid sinus hold which they all pretend to use in the ring but never do, because it puts you out in just over ten seconds and there's nothing you can do about it at all.

Twenty-Five

I WAS in my coffin. Why had they buried me face downward?

Seconds passed, and I became conscious that I was breathing. Events had been catching up with me too fast.

Was I back in the trunk of that car?

The mind moves slowly, sorting out these things. At first I believed I could see nothing, that I was pressed down upon nothing, upon velvet a hundred fathoms deep, upon the floor of a tomb. I put out my tongue, and tasted plastic, like sucking the angle of a set square in fourth-form physics class.

Sometimes the mind cannot sort things out at all.

Far-off night shapes drifted in front of my eyes, and I knew where I was. Everything that had been said and done led to this exact moment. I knew that too.

I should have done my homework. It is all very well complaining now, but there are definitions in intelligence work as precise as those I use in science, and if I'd paid more attention to Sloane I'd have known and understood those definitions weeks ago.

Tree Frog was a deception operation.

I waited for someone to speak. Logically, they had to speak. But it was only when I was sure that, after all, they wouldn't, that I'd been left alone, that this was part of it too, that I heard Andy's voice whispering in my ear.

"All right," he said. "Snap out of it. Let's go. Are you there, Yeoman?"

"I'm here," I told him. "Did you think I might have gone somewhere else?"

"That's the spirit," said Andy's voice from the tiny speaker beside my head. We hit a patch of turbulence and Tree Frog bucked slightly and then dropped a few feet. My head banged forward and down against the perspex window under my face. The slight metallic taste of blood from my lip hauled me out of the shreds of sleep.

It was a tight fit, but then Tree Frog wasn't designed for passengers, normally that is. There was a small pulling pain at the back of my left wrist and my head felt as though it had been carefully packed with plastic foam, but otherwise everything was fine. I clenched my right fist against the fuselage wall an inch or so away.

"Dylan," I said. "Just what the hell sort of license have you taken out that gives you the right to do this sort of thing to me?"

"No need to shout," said Dylan's voice. I would have torn the speaker out and crushed it to bits if I hadn't known I'd need him to talk to. "I'm wearing a headset and you're breaking my eardrums. Would you have volunteered? If we'd asked you nicely, would you have volunteered?"

"Not on your life I wouldn't," I said.

"We didn't think so. And there was rather a shortage of

qualified volunteers. You can fly, you know the hydraulic control system inside out and you know Tree Frog. We nominated you. Let's leave it at that."

"Is Driver there?" I asked.

"Sure he is."

"I'll see the lot of you frying in hell."

"Sure. We're bleeding to death about you," said Andy. "Now listen, Yeoman, you're a science boy, that means you're nice and practical. Okay, so let's all stick to getting you back alive-o and afterwards we can have a chat about the ethics and the morals, or you can sue us, or we can even arrange a short punch-up behind the gym, whatever you've got in mind."

He was right. In a situation like this I was pragmatic as the devil. I was lying on my face on a thin sheet of foam rubber. Thoughtful of them. If I looked straight down, I had a view as though I were above a bomb-aimer's window which somebody had let into the underside of the fuselage. There wasn't much to see, but the ground was too close for comfort. If I lifted my head I could see a compass and an altimeter about seven inches ahead, but that was all.

My feet were a bit warm, but then they must be practically resting on the forward end of the turbojet. I could hear the sucking whistle of air being drawn in through the intakes at about waist level each side of me. There was no sensation of moving. There never is.

As I said, it was cramped. About as cramped as crossing the Atlantic in a twelve-foot dinghy, and the outcome was likely to be just as predictable.

"Look," I said. "This thing was never meant to be flown by a live pilot."

Andy's voice crackled over the intercom. He might have been just on the other side of the bulkhead.

"So what?" he said. "It was designed for a payload of two hundred and twenty pounds of guidance equipment. You are just over one hundred and fifty pounds of guidance equipment, which means we were able to leave you the auto-pilot."

Right again. Nobody has designed a computer yet a hundredth as light or a thousandth as flexible as the human brain. It's a pity you have to haul the body it sits in around as well, but you can't have everything.

"What makes you think I can fly it?"

"Oh, come on," said Andy. "You're a hot pilot, it says so on your file. Besides you only have to fly it when you want to change course. Listen, your left arm, can you feel it?"

I explored. There was a sudden sharp dragging ache again when I moved my hand.

"We had to shove a fine polythene cannula into your dorsal vein," said Andy. "You see, we wanted to lay you out for a very precise length of time. I mean, there wouldn't be much point in ferrying you around the place asleep, and on the other hand we couldn't afford to have you wake up too soon."

"I can see that."

"Dr. Chapman worked out a gadget which drip-feeds pentothal automatically under pressure. We switched it off by remote five minutes ago, so if the tube's bothering you, pull it out."

I tried, and the tiny tube slipped out of the back of my wrist almost painlessly. There was a dressing already over the puncture, and I moved around until I could press on it for a second or two with my other hand. Moving in here was like swimming in a straitjacket. Every time I shifted the trim of the drone was upset and it lurched drunkenly. Every time, the autopilot picked it up again.

"Then what?" I asked.

"Good. Now in front of your head, if you feel around, you'll find a small control stick. It's only about three inches long, but we've rigged it to the servo-control valves in the hydraulic circuits. *Don't move it yet.*"

It was there. Just between me and the compass. I got a crick in the neck from lifting my head back to see it.

"All right, I've got it," I said.

"Right," said Andy. "Small button on top of it, okay? Now until you press that, George is still in charge."

George? Oh, George. The autopilot. Sure. My brain was still foam-wrapped but it was beginning to get a bit better. I felt around with my fingers and found the button.

"When you do press it, George takes a rest and you're on the air. You stay in control until you let it go again. If you turn onto a new course, George will keep her straight and level on that new course until you make another correction. Is that clear?"

"Yes," I told him. "The ground's a bit close for comfort right now."

"Our radar has you at five thousand feet. We've rigged you an altimeter for your own peace of mind."

I really had to laugh.

"What was that?"

"It's just that I like the bit where you're worried about my peace of mind," I said.

"Oh. Well, anyway, neither the altimeter nor the compass is one hundred percent spot on, because we didn't have time for an instrument check. It's just a lash-up really."

"Thanks," I said. "I can see you had a lot of things to attend to. Like choking me, for instance."

"Sorry about that." He didn't sound sorry. What surprised me was the way he'd changed all of a sudden from being an amiable idiot to making like a chief of staff.

"All right," said Andy. "Now get this clear. We've got you on all our radar sets here. You're flying at five thousand feet on a course one-zero-eight true. That means you're heading for the northeast corner of the Sudan. Okay? You've been fueled for seven hundred miles and you've already flown two hundred and fifty. What we want you to do is turn around, one hundred and eighty degrees, and fly back here again. It should be a cakewalk. Altitude isn't critical, only try not to fly too high. We were a little worried about oxygen when they dropped you at eleven thousand as it was. Incidentally, you've been losing height slowly and steadily since they did let go. You might try pulling her up on the stick. Have a go."

I took a deep breath and gripped the miniature joystick with the fingers of my right hand. Thumb on top, press the button. There was a rattle of clicks from somewhere below and ahead of me, which must be the autopilot disengaging. I was flying Tree Frog on my own now, and I hoped I could remember what it was like.

I pulled back cautiously and felt the nose lift. But not cautiously enough. I must have inched to the left, because at the same time I felt the plane roll slightly to port. I overcorrected in a hurry and we practically flipped over on the starboard wing.

They'd made the control too sensitive by a factor of ten or so, I thought. Far too sensitive. At the instant I realized it, I found out something else I should have recalled from looking at Tree Frog in the underground hangar at Monkham Manor. The engine wasn't exactly a ball of fire and the plane wouldn't climb steeply. I had no airspeed indicator, but I didn't need one. I could feel the controls losing bite and the nose dropped in a sickening stall.

I was still in a starboard roll. I thought for one terrible instant that we might go into a spin, and I was damn sure nobody had done proper spin trials. I couldn't tell what was happening, the whole plane felt dead and we sideslipped fast. I did the only thing I could and let go of the little control stick, and at once there was another barrage of clicks from up front as the autopilot dug us out of the mess I'd got into. The stall turned into a dive and then flattened out. I glanced at the altimeter, which was flicking about as though the needle hadn't been properly damped, but it seemed to think we were at three thousand. All I'd achieved was to lose two thousand valuable feet in height and get sick to my stomach.

"Great." Andy's voice came in my ear again. "I don't know what you're up to, but it looked terrific on our screens down here."

"Who designed this bloody gadget?" I demanded.

"What gadget's that?"

"This comic-opera control stick, of course."

"That?" He sounded surprised. I was pouring with sweat again. "Kelsey, of course, who else did you think?"

"I'll have a little word with him too. When I get back. If I get back," I said.

"You'll get back. It's your control system after all. I told you, you're unique. We might need you again."

I didn't say anything, there didn't seem to be anything much I could say without bursting a blood vessel.

"Try it again," said Andy.

I pressed the button again, moving the stick only a fraction of a millimeter this time. The aircraft lurched, but this time I held it. The altimeter needle started to crawl up the dial, hardly moving at all, but we were climbing again.

"What happens if I tell you all to go take a flying leap?" I said. "Suppose I just don't turn this thing around? It sounds unlikely I know, but just supposing I can't? What happens then?"

"You run out of gas," said Andy. "That's what happens. You should come down just about smack in the middle of the Sudanese desert. I don't know if you've looked at any maps recently, but there's even less in the way of scenery there than there is over here. Not even a camel track and two hundred miles between wells. If you see what I mean."

I saw all right. It looked as though I'd better do my best for Seeker, because they'd fixed it so that just at the moment, what was good for Seeker happened to be pretty essential for me.

"I'll come back," I said.

"Splendid. Now according to our screens you're over Sudanese territory now. I think if you feel like having a go at bringing her round, you could start turning. Don't climb and don't dive. If you move the stick to one side the hydraulic circuits will do the rest, because Kelsey tied the stick into both the aileron and the rudder circuits. Okay?"

"I hope he did it right," I said sourly. "Which way do you want me to turn?"

"Doesn't matter to us, old boy. Flip a coin if you want."

The altimeter read seven thousand now. We'd lose altitude in the turn even if I held her level. *Her?* Okay, I was emotionally bound up with Tree Frog right now. I didn't dare ask if there was a parachute anywhere around because I was afraid what the answer would be. They would tell me politely that not only was I 150 pounds of guidance equipment but that I was expendable too. I let go of the stick and the autopilot flattened out our climb and held us. Course was somewhere about one one oh according to the jury-rigged compass in front of me, a six-and-sixpenny car compass now I came to look at it closely.

I had to admit that when they made up their minds to put the fix in they did it properly. Sloane, I supposed. When you got right down and looked at it closely, it was a masterpiece, I could see that.

"What about the nice outward spiral course we were supposed to be flying according to Nockolds?" I asked.

"The theory around the station is that the drone went rogue," said Andy. His voice crackled through a haze of static. "It sometimes happens. Radio control boys are standing on their heads trying to find out what's gone wrong with their equipment. Lost you the moment you were let go from the launch, of course. They'll never work it out, but it can't be helped."

"Listen," I said. "Just how many people know I'm in this thing?"

"Nobody but just us chickens," said Andy. "Nobody at all. If they did, it might spoil the fun. Mightn't it?"

You are in the middle of a long and complicated game of poker. Nobody knows exactly who's sitting on the aces, but there's a lot of guessing going on. Nobody knows for sure whether you've got a long-range drone that you can fly in loops by radio, but you just could have, and the opposition is working up a bit of a sweat about it. The trouble is that you haven't any such thing. But that needn't stop you scooping the pool.

You arrange an exercise. In the middle of Africa. You say it's just normal short-range flight trials, baby stuff.

Before this exercise takes place, you arrange that your opponents shall be so suspicious of where you've got to in the drone business that they take various steps, such as planting an agent in your trials team. One of the reasons they're so suspicious is that you have also arranged for them to talk to a rather dim-witted scientist, who first of all says yes, we've got a nice functioning long-range drone and then changes his mind under pressure and says no, we haven't.

I would never find out who Phillips was. Flight Lieutenant Markham, I should say. Bought, or brainwashed? Or had he been a sleeper for years, waiting for just this job? It didn't matter, because Driver must have welcomed him like a long-lost brother.

Just to make doubly sure, your opponents set up a few radar surveillance posts around your trials base. They watch, listen, plot positions on maps. At the end of the exercise they know as much about the actual performance of your drone as you do. So that when it flies three hundred miles out in a straight line, does an about turn and comes smartly back again, not to mention executing a few loops, rolls and dives on the way, everybody hurries home with the news and starts to build bigger and better radar defenses, jamming devices and missiles which will home on midget glass fiber planes instead of large healthy metal ones. All of which costs money. And when, five years later, it turns out you didn't have a complicated radio control set in your drone, but just an ordinary lousy old Mark 1 human pilot, loud laughter is heard on all sides, twenty million pounds worth of defenses against a weapon that doesn't exist is scrapped, and everybody moves on to the next deal.

I made my turn to starboard. Gently, very gently. The moment I felt the plane slipping out of control I let go of everything and the autopilot straightened us up again. Then I took another bite.

I don't know what the turn looked like on radar, and it probably wasn't anywhere near as good as the radio control team could have made it, but then they were 250 miles and more out of range. When the compass read a course of two eight five, I finally let go of the control stick and lay looking downwards at the dim, moonlit ground slipping slowly beneath me.

I hoped there wasn't any wind. I never could work out drift equations.

"Fine. Terrific," Andy's voice said into my ear. "That came over just great down here on the screen."

"I didn't do it for your benefit," I told him.

"I don't suppose you did," he said. "But thanks anyway. Just what we needed."

"Glad everything's working out for you. How long before I come in to land?" I asked.

"You're three hundred miles out. Say an hour and a half. Do you want me to go through landing procedure with you?"

"No," I said. "Suppose you just leave me alone for an hour and a half. I hate to admit it, but I'm beginning to like it up here."

"Anything you say," said Andy. There was a slight pop as the carrier went off the air. The motor pushed out a steady howl behind me, and I rested my forehead on my hands and looked down onto the night desert.

It was too good to last. Twenty minutes later the carrier came on and there was a preliminary snarl of static over the speaker. I had almost gone to sleep again. They were very nearly right about it being a cakewalk, not that it made me any less keen to break somebody's neck. Landing was something I wasn't looking forward to, but I'd worry about that when the time came. In any case, I reminded myself, Tree

Frog had made dozens of landings already by itself without coming to grief.

"Control to pilot," said Andy's voice.

"Cut out the Battle of Britain talk," I said. "What's the matter now?"

"We have an unknown closing on you from the northeast."

"What does that mean?"

"Don't know yet. Estimated air speed, mach two, altitude thirty-two thousand. Range one fifty miles, closing at twelve hundred."

"So what am I supposed to do about it?" I asked.

"Not a thing," said Andy. "We just wanted to let you know, that's all. Could be Flipper, come to have a rapid shufti and then blow."

"I hope you're right," I said. "I didn't know they had any Flippers around the place up there."

The MIG-23 is a plane the *Istrebitelnya Aviatsiia Protivovozdushnoi Oborony* has been playing pretty close to the chest up to now, though they give away the 17, 19 and 21 with green stamps to the underdeveloped comrades. I wished I could go a bit faster.

"I suppose you never thought I might like to get my toe down a bit in this thing, did you?" I said. "Two hundred knots isn't exactly shaking us to pieces, you know. And at mach two he'll be here in about seven minutes flat."

"Sorry. We left the throttles set for economical cruising and called it a day," said Andy. "But don't worry, you couldn't outrun him anyway. Maybe you could give yourself another four minutes, but that's all. Relax."

"Oh sure," I said. "Supposing he feels like a little target practice?"

"He won't." There was a perceptible pause. Then, "You could dive, of course."

"You fill me with confidence," I said.

Just the same, it sounded a sensible idea. I took hold of the stick and edged it forward. The auto disengaged with its usual farrago of clicks, and Tree Frog dived. I started leveling out at fifteen hundred just in case the wings came off. I wished I'd put in some time on a few other planes besides the Anson and the Chipmunk, both excellent aircraft in their way but hardly a training ground for evading supersonic fighters.

The joke compass was still steady at two eight five. I was an hour from Al Qarif at least, in a plane which wasn't meant even remotely for this sort of thing. I counted up to about a thousand and tried to remember what the armament of the MIG-23 was. I knew it carried a pretty comprehensive line in airborne search radar and I hoped he might stick to that. Assuming it was a MIG, that is, I couldn't see it being a Convair or a Dassault, not out here. The U.A.R. were supposed to be developing a deltawing of their own, but I thought it was still in prototype form and they wouldn't be flinging it around at anywhere near mach two.

I tilted the nose down a bit more and got down to a thousand feet, but then I remembered that Andy had said the altimeter was inaccurate, and I didn't feel like pushing my luck any more. It already seemed as though I was going to bounce off the floor.

Something screamed by above my head. By the time I

heard it, it had gone, and I couldn't see overhead in any case. Inside two seconds its sound was lost against the steady background roar of Tree Frog's own turbine. I concentrated on the pattern of rocks and moon-cast shadows rushing by underneath my nose, but just the same my head hunched into my shoulders in reflex, pointless protection.

At the height I was above ground level I must be pretty difficult to see against the desert floor and almost impossible to pick up on his intercept radar. I was probably beneath Al Qarif's radar horizon too, if it came to that. I was invisible, and that meant I was as good as dead if Charlie boy up there decided to get trigger happy and risk an unprovable incident.

I shouted into the intercom, but all I got was interference. There was another roar above me as Charlie boy came to take a closer look. He couldn't slow down to my air speed without coming pretty close to stalling and nobody in their right minds would risk a stall this close to the ground. I kept my fingers crossed and waited for the roar of his engine to pull out ahead of me. Then I grabbed the tiny control stick and turned to port, trying to gain a little altitude at the same time without making my first mistake all over again and getting into sideslip, because if I did I might never get out of it this time. I wanted more than anything to be able to see what the hell was going on above me, but I couldn't. Maybe it was just as well, since there was nothing I could do about it.

A dome of rock humped its back underneath the perspex window and seemed to brush past the end of my nose. I levered the stick back a fraction more, climbing to eighteen hundred feet by the altimeter. I was still turning port, which meant that at last I was beginning to get the hang of flying this thing. Suddenly Andy's voice came in again on the crash of atmospherics.

"Are you okay?" He was two hundred miles away. What could he do if I wasn't?

"Andy," I said. "Flaps and skids. How do I put them down?"

"You can't, not yet. You'll never make it back here with the extra drag."

I was in no real mood for argument.

"The flaps, Andy. The flaps," I said. "Never mind about getting home. I don't want to plough into the sand out here at about two hundred knots on my belly."

"There's a bar switch at the base of the control stick," he said. "It brings in the auxiliary hydraulics and the system will look after the rest for you. But you can't go in to land now."

"You argue it out with Charlie boy," I said. "He keeps buzzing me and I don't know whether he's just doing it for laughs. Have you got me on radar?"

"Yes. Charlie boy too. He's just coming up behind you on another circuit. Giles—"

"Get lost," I said.

I could hear him coming in again overhead. He must have thought he was going round the bend. Assuming he could get a proper look at me, he wouldn't be able to see any cockpit, so he must assume he was looking at a drone. I went into a dive again. Perhaps he was trying to make a guess at our length, and that would give him an even bigger headache.

I heard him barreling by on my starboard. I still couldn't get a glimpse of him, and unless he was a real hotshot and flew directly underneath me I never would. He was close enough on that pass to rock the drone with his wash, and I'd had enough. I'd have to go in and land while I could choose what I was doing, within limits. Charlie boy could probably chop us in half and never notice. I hoped he wouldn't get too keen.

I felt around the base of the column until I found the bar switch Andy had said was there. We were still in a shallow dive and I could see an open stretch of sand ahead. It would have to do, I couldn't go on doing low-altitude aerobatics forever.

I pressed the bar with my thumb and there was a whine as the auxiliary turbine fired and drove the flaps and skids down. The increased drag slowed the plane down and felt as though it was shaking me to pieces, never mind the airframe. The nose dipped still more. I didn't know what Charlie boy was doing, I had enough on my plate. I was too far from home, I didn't want to land with enough spare fuel on board for another two hundred miles and most particularly I didn't want to land with the turbojet still running, but that was just too bad. I had no means of switching off and the only way to cut the motor was to touch down and let the automatic contact switch on the plane's belly cut it for me.

I flattened out. It looked as though the first thing to hit the ground would be my face. The flaps must have pulled us down to something like a hundred but it was still a lot too fast. I peered down and back through the plastic window, and I could just see that the forward end of the belly skid was down. Then the ground poured towards me in a rush and I let go of everything and buried my face in my arms.

I felt us touch. The sting switch cut the engine at once and slammed the flaps back into the trailing edges of the wings to stop the plane bouncing. As it was we seemed to float like a skimming stone for about a hundred miles and then we were ripping into the sand and the deceleration shoved my head forward into the little control stick. I found there was a safety harness around my waist. They'd thought of everything. Everything except whether press-gang ethics were out of place these days or not, but I don't suppose they lay awake at nights much worrying about ethical problems.

I was lucky. The ground was harder than I'd have thought, but not too hard. The tail skid dug its claws in and dragged us to a halt.

There was a hot, sticky silence. I realized I'd forgotten to ask how I was supposed to get out of this thing, but I tried to think back to Monkham Manor and Kelsey removing the access panels. I groped around above my head. Then I realized I'd never do it that way either and I fought my way onto my back, unclipping the safety harness around my waist. The smell of hot engine was growing stronger every second and although the odds were against all that kerosene catching fire I didn't want to hang around.

I found the inside fasteners, and thirty seconds later I was chinning myself into the open air. I tore my shirt on the edge of the access hatch, and when I was almost out Tree Frog tipped onto her port wing and I slithered to the ground down the fuselage, ungracefully and upside down. I didn't give a damn. It was just enough to be able to stand upright again.

There was a rumble in the sky and for an instant I wondered what it was. I'd forgotten all about Charlie boy, and I crouched down again and saw the delta shape thunder across overhead. He couldn't possibly have seen me in any case, but I stayed still while he came round again for the last time and then swept off towards the north. Then I got up and walked away from the plane, the fine gravel giving under my feet like a quicksand.

The crystal of my watch was cracked, but it was still going. I held it to my ear and listened to its tick. It was three o'clock.

Everybody must know more or less where I was, so all I had to do was sit tight and wait.

Twenty-Six

It was cold, as it always is at night, so after twenty minutes I went back and leaned against Tree Frog. There must be about fifty gallons of fuel left in the tanks, but by now I was past caring whether it caught fire or exploded or simply did nothing at all.

At half past three I climbed back and slid head and shoulders inside the fuselage. I found the speaker of the intercom and said 'hello' into it a few times, but there was no reply and no static crackle either. I didn't think there would be. I felt around to see if they'd been thoughtful enough to leave me a canteen of water, but of course they hadn't and I didn't really expect that either. I was supposed to come back like a good boy and land within five miles of Al Qarif, and since I hadn't done so, presumably it was my own stupid fault. I jumped down off the wing root again and started to think about search parties.

If they had me pinned to within ten miles or so when I landed they could send out a search plane as soon as it got light. Or they could start even before that with a truck, since they were probably more interested in Tree Frog than me.

Now I came to think of it nobody (at least according to Andy) knew I was here except Seeker and Kelsey and hence probably Nockolds, and if they wanted to keep things on that footing they'd have to be pretty cagey about whom and what they sent out to pick me up. It would be interesting to see how they handled that one.

My back was warm where it rested against the fuselage, but my feet were getting cold. I wasn't dressed for desert survival. Until the sun came up I was laughing, but after that I knew it would be downhill all the way.

I stood up and stamped my feet in the yielding grit to bring the circulation back into them. It looked as though I was somewhere near the edge of a *reg*, one of the huge flat plains of gravel which are, more than anything, the true desert. Over to the east was a jumble of broken rock and then a round outcrop, presumably the one I'd flown over while Charlie boy was taking a good look at me. It was about five miles away, or maybe ten, I couldn't tell. The moon was setting and it would soon be even darker than it was now.

To the west and north there was nothing but desolate, flat ground for as far as I could see. I began to think of walking towards the rocks while it was still cool, but I knew I had to stay by Tree Frog or I'd never be found. It was murder plodding around in the gravel, so I gave up and went back to where the plane lay like a crucifix, dark against the glinting, wind-polished stones, and sat down again.

Something was moving towards me, slowly, from the west. It was just after sunrise, but already I was beginning to prickle with warmth. They should be arriving to pick me up by now, and I kept my eyes on the dark dot far away on the horizon. I was sitting in the shadow cast by the starboard wing. One lens of my sunglasses was cracked where I'd rolled on it in my hip pocket, but I was lucky to have them with me at all. I felt thirsty already, not because I was dehydrated but simply because there wasn't anything to drink. I told myself firmly that thirst was a state of mind, but it didn't do me a blind bit of good.

It must be a fairly small vehicle. It seemed hardly to have moved in the last twenty minutes. A light pickup, perhaps a Land Rover.

If Andy Dylan was driving it, I wouldn't break his bloody neck so long as he'd remembered to bring a bottle of beer. He owed me a drink, one way and another, and I couldn't think of a better time to take it off him.

If it was Driver I'd break his neck anyway.

Twenty-Seven

THE truck rolled to a halt about ten yards away. I squinted against the reflected glare from the wind-screen, shading my eyes with my hand. There was something about the truck which wasn't quite right, but I was damned if I was getting up.

A man climbed out of the cab. He was dressed for Lawrence of Arabia, white shirt, K.D.'s and a blue-striped *burnous* over the lot. There was a pistol stuck in the waistband of the trousers. He was about Andy's build, but it wasn't Andy. I sat upright, bumping my head on the underside of the wing.

"Good morning," said Pzenica. "I am very glad to find you here. But where is your truck, please?"

I should have remembered there were whole crowds of people over to the west besides us. And their radar was just as accurate. I was surprised to see it was Pzenica who'd come out, but he was obviously right in his element.

"My truck?" I asked stupidly.

"Yes. Or have they left you here on guard while they make arrangements to collect the plane?"

I wasn't supposed to be here at all, of course. But it was too late to think about that now. In any case there was no place I could have hidden. Not within ten miles.

Pzenica strolled over and tapped Tree Frog on the nose with his finger. He bent down and picked up the access hatch cover, which was lying under the port wing, and felt its weight thoughtfully. He peered inside the fuselage. He was finding it pretty hard to take himself, but he was coming round to the idea in the end.

"You . . . were flying in this thing? It is impossible," he said.

"Ridiculous," I agreed.

"Nevertheless." He was beginning to sound like Christopher Greve-Gillett. He dived back into the access hatch and then straightened up to look at me. "Not very comfortable, I should say." He grinned. "You clever bastard. You clever, clever bastard."

"Don't look at me. It wasn't my idea," I said.

"But you *were* flying it, no?" He went around to the tail. "Tree Frog," he said. "Well, well, well." He looked into the tailpipe and felt the lining. It was probably still warm. "I am filled with admiration," he said. He strode back to the truck and came back with a canteen.

"You must be thirsty," he said. "I would drink your health, but unfortunately I have only water." He held the canteen out to me. I began to feel like a captured air ace in the days of the R.F.C.

"Water will do just fine," I told him. I took the canteen and tilted it back into my mouth. It was getting on for the best drink I've ever tasted, though there was a flavor of sulphur about it just like the water at Al Qarif.

I handed the canteen back to him and he wiped the mouth and drank himself. The only thing I could think of was to keep him here until Seeker's representative arrived, whoever that might be. I didn't know what they'd do about him, but that wasn't my affair.

"You should not be standing in the sun with your head uncovered," said Pzenica. "You will get sunstroke. I shall find you something to wear on your head, if you excuse me."

"It's a fallacy," I told him. He didn't believe me. He reached into the pocket of his trousers and handed me a large silk handkerchief. I draped it over my head out of politeness. He climbed on top of the fuselage again and looked inside the space I'd occupied. It only occurred to me later that he could see I wasn't carrying a gun and was just checking to see if I'd left one behind in the plane. He emerged again, smiling and shaking his head.

"A very tight fit," he said. "Well. It is a little different from the last time I saw you." He waved his hand around at all the sand. He was right; last time I'd been in three feet of snow. It felt as though it were about a century ago.

"I do not have to tell you that I am very sorry about what happened to you," he went on. "Also about . . . I am sorry, I cannot remember her name. The girl with you, the *jolie laide*. These things happen. No bad feelings, I hope. By the way you nearly shot me, also you did shoot Lenk but he is better now."

"Oh, good," I said. It seemed just about to cover it.

"I expect you wonder how I happen to be here before your friends," said Pzenica. He sat down on the ground and motioned me politely to take a seat beside him. "The truth is that we have been following your plane on radar, though of course you could not know this."

"The world is full of surprises," I said.

"Yes," he said. "We found it very difficult to believe the evidence of our own eyes, particularly when you were avoiding that other plane. Now of course everything is clear, very clear. I expect the others up there were puzzled too," he pointed over towards the northeast. "That is why they sent out the plane you avoided and which, no doubt, forced you to land here."

"Oh," I said. "That wasn't your lot?"

"Our lot? No, of course not." He seemed surprised. I had no doubt it would come to the same thing in the end, however they pooled their information. Unless Kiess was running his group purely as a private enterprise, which seemed unlikely. I wished I disliked Pzenica. He seemed to have that particular form of cheerful lunacy which was so conspicuously lacking in, say, Kiess. Or Driver. I knew perfectly well that he'd blow a hole in me a foot wide just as soon as it suited him to do so, but I still found it hard to dislike him.

"This Tree Frog," he said. "It must be very difficult to fly? It cannot have been designed with such an idea in mind."

I didn't answer. I couldn't see what the outcome of this would be, but meanwhile I was going to keep my mouth shut.

"I am sorry, I did not mean to discuss things with you if you would rather not," said Pzenica. After a moment or two he went on, "It surprises me that you told nothing of this to Maxius. I was sure you were telling the truth. In the end I believed you were sufficiently disorientated. It is unwise to be too confident of one's technique. But I was sure you were telling the truth."

"I'll let you into a secret," I said. "I was pretty sure I was telling the truth myself." He laughed. The English always make the joke, I could see that.

"Perhaps you are, after all, a professional?" He settled himself back against the fuselage. This was where I made a grab for his gun and held him up until the cavalry arrived, except it was too early for that sort of thing.

"We, of course, are all professionals," he said. "In Poland, from children we are all professionals. The Germans, and then the Russians, you understand, you can see how it must be. The fascists and then the communists. If one wishes to stay in the middle," he pressed his palms together in emphasis, "then one learns certain skills from a very early age. This is not true in England, I think, you have too many elections."

"Perhaps we do," I said. I looked over to the west. Surely somebody must be coming by now. He would see them as soon as I did, of course.

"You will realize that I am not a properly educated man," he said.

"You've written several research papers," I pointed out.

"Oh, that. Research? This can be performed by anybody with . . ." he tapped the side of his head.

"Brains?"

"No, not brains, that is not the word I want."

"Commonsense."

"Exactly. Anybody with commonsense. You do not think?"

I was surprised to see this view of scientific research was spreading so fast. Both sides of the Iron Curtain, it seemed.

"Well," said Pzenica. "I have been very pleased to talk with you, but I am afraid we must go now. I am fifty miles ahead of your friends at Al Qarif, but they cannot be very long, can they?"

He stood up. The *burnous* was swept back at his waist. He was too gentlemanly to start waving guns around before it was absolutely necessary, but he was making sure I got the message. I stood up beside him and walked over to the truck. He followed casually. He was hardly worried, since there wasn't, after all, any place I could run to.

I had known all the time that it would come to this, but it was clearer than ever now. I had to stop him not merely from taking me back with him, but from getting away at all. Even if it meant killing him.

Otherwise everything that had been done up to now was wasted. As a matter of fact, if he had a radio in the truck and got as far as picking up the transmitter and telling whoever was listening at the other end that he'd found me here, we were cooked. As far as I was concerned the whole thing might be a totally pointless exercise in cold-war espionage, but the fact remained that if Pzenica got back to base we might just as well never have started.

I tried to make myself believe that it mattered. I walked around to the far side of the truck and opened the door. Just as he got near, I leaned in and took the ignition key out, casually, looked around the cab and then straightened up.

"Nobody's going anywhere," I said.

"But don't be stupid," he said. "You are not armed."

He seemed to be genuinely concerned, as though he were explaining to me the simple rules of the game that everybody knew already and which ought to be obvious even to outsiders. The man with the gun gave the instructions, and you obeyed them until you were the man with the gun and the positions were reversed. If anybody declined to obey the rules, the mortality rate would be unnecessarily high, and to a professional this would be untidy.

I shook my head. We were looking at each other through both open doors of the cab. He put his hand on the butt of the gun.

"Please, Dr. Yeoman."

I didn't move. He came round the front of the truck, quite slowly. As he drew the gun and rounded the wing on my side of the cab, I swung the spanner I'd picked up with the ignition key and which I'd kept hidden from his line of sight. It was a four-centimeter heavy-duty wrench and it must have damn nearly broken his wrist. The pistol flew out of his hand and landed ten feet behind him, over toward Tree Frog.

As he turned I jumped past him. He was holding his wrist with his left hand and he didn't move quickly enough, and I got my foot to the gun as it lay on the gravel and kicked it hard. I watched it skate along the gravel and come to rest under Tree Frog's wing.

I felt as though I were in one of those nightmares which

glue your feet to the ground, in which you move as fast as you can and yet cannot move at all. Stones showered over us as we dived for the gun together, and I hoped his wrist was broken, because if it was maybe I could get the gun in my hand first and he'd see sense better than I had. Maybe it was the only advantage the amateur had over the professional in this game, unwillingness to go by the obvious rules.

He kicked me off the gun by aiming his foot at my face, and I put up my hands and rolled back to protect myself. Then he was down on top of me and by the time I'd recovered balance he was holding it by the muzzle and was fighting to get it the right way round in his hand. I drove my fingers at his eyes. Somebody once told me that the real deterrent is to stick your fingers in your enemy's nostrils and tear outward, splitting the nose back to the cartilage, but it took more precision than I was capable of. I needed practice. I had time to see that it was one of the Parabellum models, the FN or the Stechkin perhaps, even the Luger if they were still around, and then it went off.

The circle of the muzzle was pointing straight at me, I thought. I couldn't see how it hadn't killed me, and at the same instant there was a noise like a grenade going off above and behind me. Aviation kerosene was safe enough, but there was still the little auxiliary turbine and he must have hit the nitro tank. I dived over him and rolled clear. Pzenica didn't understand what had happened, he was still concentrating on the gun. I jackknifed out from under the wing and as I did so the plane rolled over towards me and pinned his robe under the fuselage. He still couldn't see the danger. I heard myself yell at him and I tried to get back under the wing and heave it up to free him, but I don't think he even knew he was trapped. He swung the gun around and fired at me again.

There was a gigantic, numbing shock in my shoulder which spun me back and away, sprawling me on the sand. Before I could even move there was a second, louder explosion, probably the oxidant and the kerosene boiling together this time, and the blackish, carbon-laden smoke and flame I knew from all the crashes I'd gone to licked out in greasy ten-foot tongues towards me and I crawled away across the sand and never heard him scream. I hope the oxidant tank killed him when it blew. I believe it did.

Heat rippled the air like watered silk. I fitted the key into the truck's dash and backed off about thirty yards, while Tree Frog burned to a shell, the glass fiber buckling and splitting in a machinegun rattle of hot exploding stones.

Twenty-Eight

THERE had been very little water in the canteen to start with, and now there was none. I'd used the last few drops to soak the handkerchief Pzenica had given me against the sun, and which was now rolled and wadded into my left shoulder. Blood was returning to the numbed flesh there and it hurt like hell.

I sat in the truck with both cab doors open. It was the only way I could keep the interior temperature within bearable limits, and the outside air drifted through, still slightly tainted with smoke, and made me retch.

Three hours had passed. Once I heard the drone of a single-engined aircraft away to the north, but I couldn't see it and no signal I could make would add anything to the burned-out cross of the plane against the sand. I no longer believed anyone was coming to pick me up, and it hardly seemed to matter.

The truck was facing east, away from the plane. The rocks on the horizon gave me something to fix my eyes on. The green roof of the cab filtered out some of the sun. In an hour or so, I knew, I would stop waiting for help to arrive. I would start the engine and drive away from the place. I had reached the point where I had lost interest, and when you reach that point in the desert you are already dead.

We all draw ourselves pictures of the way we think we ought to look. All of us. Then, slowly, we begin to change, to conform to these caricatures, so that the barber becomes more barberlike and the managing director becomes distilled essence of managing director. For most of us, this process only occurs during the day, while we are at work, and in the evening and on weekends we fold the picture away and revert, almost, to what we really are. But in the Secret Service the day is twenty-four hours long, and there is no such thing as a return to normal. After a year or two, the picture takes over completely, I could see that now. Kiess and Sloane had turned into their own silhouettes of power, operating the theory of games on some obscure level, as a discipline. Driver must at some time have seen himself as the bluff, pipe-smoking man of action, and because nobody was around to tell him to give it a rest for a bit, he had set into the posture like concrete.

I put my right hand up, the one I could move, and rested the back of it for an instant on the roof. I drew it back, and the hairs were scorched. Some time soon, my own cooling system would break down and I would stop sweating and, in a short while, die. I don't know what Andy Dylan saw himself as, perhaps he hadn't been in the trade long enough to sort himself out a blueprint. Pzenica had seen himself as Rudolph Rassendyl, the gentleman of fortune, and he was dead, which probably showed how much percentage there was in being a gentleman of fortune when it came to the push.

I shifted my weight against the back of the bucket seat, and pain tore through my shoulder. I could feel a trickle of blood running down the inside of my arm, but there wasn't much I could do about it. The shot had taken me too high in the shoulder for a tourniquet. There were all sorts of things I should be doing. Running through pages one to ten of the Desert Survival Manual, or looking for snails like that dedicated lad at Farnborough had proved were just the thing if you couldn't get hold of steak. I tried to recall how many of the things he'd found out you had to collect in order to stay alive, but in any case I was in no shape for snail-hunting.

The red and grey rocks to the east ahead of me changed shape and color, became camels, rearranged themselves into Stonehenge, marched towards me and slid away ten thousand miles. I couldn't tell if I was thirsty or not, which was interesting but of no great importance. When Yancy rolled up in the ice-cream van it hardly surprised me at all.

"Hello, Yance," I said. "The plane's burned out so there's nothing left to see."

"So I notice," said Yancy. "Where's the guy you grabbed this truck off?"

"He's dead."

"Okay," said Yancy. "You can tell me about it later."

It seemed in a way to sum up our relations with the Americans in general. Everybody knows we were burning the cakes and writing madrigals while there was nothing across the Atlantic except buffalo. It's universally admitted (in

British scientific circles anyway) that the only reason they are ahead in the U. S. is because all their research departments have million-dollar project grants, while we carry on discovering nuclear fission with an air of nonchalance, a ten-shilling budget and a short length of string. All this is beyond dispute and has been for as long as I remember. But I was in the middle of the Sahara with a bullet wound in the left shoulder and death in delirium a short ride over the hill, and Yancy Brightwell had rolled up, not just with an ambulance but a refrigerated truck.

Mohammed Jalil al Murzuq drove us home at a frightening sixty, and I lay in the back of the truck and smoked one of Yancy's cigarettes, thinking of Pzenica's face and the wide blue circle of the Parabellum exploding into my eyes.

Yancy sat opposite me, apparently weighed down by some sort of grievance. He was wearing boxing boots, a mud-green baseball cap and hexagonal frameless polaroids. He looked like the sort of thing Wing Commander Baker dreamed about after a heavy cheese and lobster dinn

"That magnesium alloy," he said.

"What about it?"

"Wicked stuff," he said. "It sure gets a hold on things when it catches. What's left of that plane isn't worth raking through for clinker, you know that?"

"I know," I said. "I saw it burn."

"Quite a bit of engine left, of course, and a few square feet of tail structure, but aside from that you did a good job."

"It wasn't me," I told him. "I suppose you could say it was an accident."

"Yes," said Yancy. "Some accident, though."

"Sorry you came all that way for nothing. By the way," I asked him, "what brought you out at all? I'd like to think Driver sent you, except that just talking to you at all is high treason according to him."

He lit me another cigarette. The truck slewed round as we hit a stretch of loose sand and my left shoulder nearly came out of its socket, but Mohammed was going too fast to get bogged down. I tried to work out whether, from start to finish of this thing, I'd traveled more mileage as a passenger or as freight. There couldn't be much in it.

"You catch on pretty slow, don't you?" he said. "What do you think I was doing while you were up there batting around the sky? Sitting on my fat?"

If Driver and Nockolds had really wanted him where they could keep an eye on him, they should have gone the whole hog and had him inside the radome or the control trailer.

"Tell me," I said, "is there anybody around here who *hasn't* been watching this operation on their little radar screens?"

"I doubt it. Couple of the emergent nations may have been tuned in on Fight of the Week instead, I guess. There isn't much of the sky left as private property these days." He turned and looked through the window into the cab to see where we were. When he turned back I could see he was smiling. "Tell you something really funny, though," he started. Then he changed his mind. "Come to think of it, maybe I just better keep my big mouth shut." He leaned over me. "If you want to pass out, feller," he said, "that's okay with me."

I wasn't sure whether to take him up on it or not. The wound was starting to itch, but he'd done such an efficient first-aid job that I couldn't reach it to do anything about it. I shut my eyes and lay there feeling the truck sway and buck over the sand. I hoped the bullet hadn't done as much damage as I believed. One thing I was quite certain of. When I got back there was going to be a stack of trouble for the laughing lads at Seeker.

Twenty-Nine

INSIDE Station Sick Quarters the temperature was down to ninety. They X-rayed my shoulder, and the M.O. told me he didn't think he wanted to mess around with extracting the bullet, if I agreed. I agreed all right. A 9 mm. round at six feet packs a lot of kinetic energy and it all goes somewhere on impact. I didn't want anyone spending the next six hours picking out bone splinters without a nice expensive operating theater with all the accessories to back them up.

He looked as though there were half a dozen things he wanted to ask me, but he didn't ask any of them.

Hendrickson, the Station Intelligence Officer, arrived at about four in the afternoon. He said they'd laid on a transport plane leaving at six, for Sebha and Tunis, and he hoped I'd be comfortable. He told me I'd had a bit of a rough time. I thanked him, and he came closer, looking over his shoulder as though he thought somebody would come in and catch him.

"Just what did happen out there?" he asked.

"I'm afraid I haven't quite got the full hang of it. Not yet." He sounded aggrieved. In my view he had every right to be.

"What's your security rating?" I asked him.

"Don't follow you, old boy," he said. "Same as everybody else's in this flyblown sand-trap."

"Ah," I said. "Then I don't think I should tell you anything without the express permission of my superiors. Except that the shores of Albion have been relieved of a dreadful peril."

"Bloody funny, old boy."

He got up and started towards the door. "All I say is that I think somebody might have put me in the picture," he said. "After all I'm the poor bloody intelligence wallah around here."

I beckoned him back, and he came around to the other side of the bed.

"I'll tell you a secret," I said. "I think somebody ought to have put me in the picture too." The door opened and Driver and Chapman came in, and a minute later Hendrickson left.

"If you think I'm going to stand at ease with a smile on my face while you put in some comic-opera report about all this, you've got another think coming," I said. Driver made a small deprecating movement with his hand as though this were something we could all sort out later over a pint. It wasn't, I wanted to get it through to him.

"I'll tell you something else," I went on. "I had plenty of time to think out there. And you know the conclusion I came to? You're psychotic, the lot of you. You live in some fantasy life which lets you think it's quite normal to cook up a ludicrous scheme like this, and then bend everybody within range around just so that they fit it."

Chapman blinked once or twice. He appeared to be considering this.

"I'll concede the point to you," he said finally. "Except that I must disagree with you on rather philosophical grounds. The true test of madness, if there is one at all, consists in asking whether or not the subject is coping adequately with the world he lives in or not. If he does not, we label him psychotic. I think, if you consider the matter, Dr. Yeoman, you will find that we cope perfectly well. You might even say we were mentally adapted to do so."

He beamed at me indulgently, and I could see that he was absolutely right. In peace, the hooligan is a public menace. In wartime, he is at a premium. This has of course been pointed out before. All you had to remember was that Driver and Chapman had been at war all their lives and always would be at war, and it made sense.

"Why was it Yancy Brightwell who came out and picked me up?" I asked.

"Ah," said Chapman. "I'm afraid you aren't going to like this very much, Yeoman, but the fact is that we didn't know exactly where you were. You were supposed to come to within five or ten miles before landing. Indeed, if you had done so, we could have saved you a good deal of trouble."

"Tough," I said. "What do you mean, you didn't know exactly where I was? You were tracking me."

"We lost you about seven minutes before you landed and according to where Captain Brightwell says he picked you up you must have turned to port instead of flying in a straight line."

"You *lost* me? On radar?"

"I'm afraid so. No doubt it had something to do with the fact that ostensibly the drone went out of control, which is what the radar and control crews believed. They were already searching for faults before your echo went below horizon. One of those things, I'm afraid. We would of course have found you, but when we heard Captain Brightwell was picking you up, it didn't seem necessary to intervene."

I thought this over. No wonder Yancy was practically breaking in half laughing. Everybody had been glued tight onto Tree Frog's progress and mine, except the men in charge. I wished I felt more like laughing myself. I also hoped Yancy had got enough of what he wanted out of Tree Frog, because I reckoned he deserved it.

At ten to six I heard the Pioneer's engines coughing into life outside on the strip. The screen doors batted apart and Kelsey and Nockolds came in.

"That control stick, Kel," I said.

"What about it?"

"Too sensitive. Every time I touched the damn thing we rolled all over the sky," I told him. He was very interested.

"Yes. We saw that on the screen. I was quite worried for a bit until I saw you'd got the hang of it," he said. "The difficulty was that there wasn't any real way of flight testing it in the circumstances, so I just had to hope you knew your own hydraulic valves best."

I wanted to ask them both why the hell they thought it

was a good idea, even a permissible idea, to stick me into the air in an inadequately tested drone with a totally untested control system. I wanted to hear Kelsey's views, in particular, about the ethics involved. But I wasn't given the chance.

"Very fine show," said Nockolds briskly. "I don't want to make too much of a song and dance about it of course, but it was a damn fine show on your part. I wouldn't have done it myself."

I forgot all about the shoulder, at least until I'd sat upright.

"You thought I volunteered," I said at last. Then, "Or at least, that's the way you've decided to play it."

They looked at me as though they hadn't quite heard, and the thin whisper of an idea began to creep in on me.

"You thought Seeker put in an ad for a hero?" I said. "To get shoehorned into that flying mummy-case and throw it around the sky for the benefit of your lot? Is that what you thought?"

"Well, naturally," said Nockolds.

"Naturally, nothing," I said. "It was a case of everybody else one step backward march. From start to end nobody gave me the slightest idea of what went on and I hadn't got the brains to work it out for myself. If I had, you wouldn't have been able to see me from here with the Palomar reflector."

"I can hardly believe you're serious," said Nockolds. But I was watching Kelsey, and I remembered the way he tried to avoid me all the time I'd been at Al Qarif, and I saw him again, vanishing into the darkness just after he'd wished me luck. What had I said? "It's nothing to do with me." Kelsey knew I'd been set up for it all right, but there was nothing I could say about it now.

"Okay. I'm just having febrile nightmares, Kel," I said. "Next time you design a control column, consult me first, will you? It's my line of country, or didn't you know?"

The screens banged open again and a stretcher party came in, so I didn't have the time I needed to follow it up. "No thanks," I told the medical orderly, "I'll walk. I've been ferried around too much for my own good just recently."

"Whatever you like, sir," the orderly said. It was nothing to him how the civilians acted up. Halfway across to the Pioneer I began to regret I'd started it, but at least I was under my own steam, which made a change.

Back in London, they got me into the Lindo Wing at St. Mary's, which was v.i.p. treatment all right. I don't know how long it took them to jigsaw the bits of my shoulder together, but after three days it was just beginning to be comfortable. I lay in bed and read half a column-inch in the *Guardian* describing recent and successful pilotless aircraft trials and drawing comfort from the fact that once again we were leading the world. That was on page six, but on page one aeronautical engineers were still leaving in droves for America. Maybe Yancy had spread the word around. The last person I wanted to see was Andy Dylan, in blazer and flannels this time and looking at peace with the world for once.

"What's the matter, did they promote you?" I asked him. "You mean Driver wasn't upset you goofed off with the radar just towards the end?"

"Everybody's pretty happy about the whole exercise, thanks," he said.

"Everybody except me."

"Come on," he said. "Aren't you even the least bit pleased they're having a special medal struck for you?"

"That depends on what's in the citation and where they're going to pin it," I said. "Just tell Driver from me that my expenses claim is going to make even Seeker blink this time. Believe me."

"I don't know about that," he said. "People up top sometimes ask questions, you know."

"Surprise me some more."

"As a matter of fact it's about the only thing they ever do question," he said. "If you see what I mean." He looked around the room, which was done in a delicate pastel green. "Nice," he said. "Does the television come on the house?"

"No," I told him. "You're paying for it. You'll find out."

"So long as it keeps you happy. We don't want any complaints."

"You're joking again," I said. "You don't really think I'm going to sit around and say nothing, do you?"

He sighed. I could see that I hadn't come up to specification again. He offered me a cigarette and helped himself to an apple in exchange. "Do yourself a favor, Giles," he said.

"Not a hope," I told him. "I'm going to scream my head off, starting from habeas corpus and finishing at life, liberty and the pursuit of happiness. You may have got this whole thing buttoned up, but I'm going to find out just how firmly."

He bit into the apple with a crunch.

"The assistant to the Second Secretary is coming to see

you," he said. "He'll listen to anything you may feel like telling him."

"Oh, yes?" I said.

The assistant to the Second Secretary, inevitably, had Christopher Greve-Gillett with him.

"I am asked by the Minister to thank you," he said. He looked out of the window at the scaffolding which stops St. Mary's collapsing into Paddington Goods Depot. "Of course we knew we could rely on you from the Moroccan business."

I said nothing.

"Very grateful for your offer of help," he went on. "They tell me you'll be out of here in a few days. I imagine you'll be taking some sort of holiday, won't you?"

"I hadn't got around to thinking about it yet," I said. "But yes, I suppose I might."

He looked at Greve-Gillett, who took over, which meant studying the floor carefully before committing himself to the spoken word. "If you were thinking of going abroad," he said finally, "you'd keep us posted, wouldn't you? Just as a matter of form."

"I thought of going to Wales," I said. "I don't think I can be much of an embarrassment there, do you?"

"Of course not," said Greve-Gillett. "I didn't mean to imply."

When they'd stayed long enough to satisfy protocol and were almost halfway through the door, I stopped them.

"This is off the record." They turned round. "I just want to make sure you get this into the mental filing system," I said. "I was press-ganged. Is that quite clear? I made no offer of help, or none that would include what happened out there at Al Qarif. Have you got that quite clear? I realize you probably know it already, but just in case there's any doubt about it, you understand?"

"But this is most serious," said the assistant to the Second Secretary.

"No," I said. "It's not serious, and we all know it. Because even if it was serious, nothing whatever would be done about it." He looked as though he were going to start another semi-official protest, but I wasn't interested. "Just pass the word around, that's all I ask," I said to them. "Next time, go trundle it somewhere else. That's the message."

The next morning Binnie arrived. She'd been on holiday in Pembrokeshire, but now she had a stack of files under her arm and a letter from the Institute. The files were all labeled Flittermouse and the letter said no dice, no computer, no Admiralty grant for time in lieu. I told her to pass the lot on to McTeague, and she stayed till six.